CRY UNCLE

A J. McNee Mystery

Russel D. McLean

Severn House Large Print
London & New York

This first large print edition published 2016
in Great Britain and the USA by
SEVERN HOUSE PUBLISHERS LTD of
19 Cedar Road, Sutton, Surrey, England, SM2 5DA.
First world regular print edition published 2014 by
Severn House Publishers Ltd., London and New York.

British Library Cataloguing in Publication Data

McLean, Russel D. author.
   Cry uncle. – (A J. McNee mystery ; 5)
   1. McNee, J. (Fictitious character)–Fiction. 2. Murder–
Investigation–Scotland–Dundee–Fiction. 3. Dundee
(Scotland)–Fiction. 4. Detective and mystery stories.
   5. Large type books.
   I. Title II. Series
   823.9'2-dc23

ISBN-13: 9780727870100

Severn House Publishers support the Forest Stewardship Council™
[FSC™], the leading international forest certification organisation. All
our titles that are printed on FSC certified paper carry the FSC logo.

MIX
Paper from
responsible sources
FSC® C013056

Typeset by Palimpsest Book Production Ltd.,
Falkirk, Stirlingshire, Scotland.
Printed and bound in Great Britain by
T J International, Padstow, Cornwall.

*This one's for
Al Guthrie
Secret Agent Man, Blasted Heathen, Master
of Noir. And without him, McNee would
never have made it to publication at all,
never mind lasted for five books.
Thank you.*

Dundee 2012

The old man kneels before me. Spreads his arms. Lowers his head. Showing regret for what he has done? Or acceptance for what he knows has to happen?

'Do it, then, you prick.'

I'm shaking. My breath is shallow. Staccato. Something in my chest vibrates with every puff of my lungs.

After all these years, it ends here.

Like it began. In the rain. Blood mixing with water. Unspoken anger. Another man waiting for me to decide his fate.

I was ready to kill a man then.

Do I still have that within me?

Or have I changed?

The rain batters down. We're both soaked through. The water rivulets down my face, gets in my eyes, obscures my vision.

Over the noise, the old man says, 'This is what you wanted all along. Do it.'

I lock my arm. Committing. My fingers snake around the grip, index extending to the guard.

The gun trembles.

I think to myself, that after all this time, I have to do this. For everyone the old man killed. Directly. Indirectly. For every injustice carried out in his name, under his orders.

Whether or not the old anger burns, from a

1

pure and pragmatic point of view the world is better off without men like David Burns.

He deserves this.

No trial. No jail time. No cushy, gentle death as a guest at Her Majesty's pleasure. No, not for David Bloody Burns. He was always going to die like this. Maybe not with me at the other end of the gun, but someone. Someone who hated him. Who understood what they were doing. Whose actions were justified. Maybe not in the eyes of the law, but under a grander and greater kind of justice.

The old man isn't afraid. Acting like he welcomes death. And maybe he does. Maybe he's prepared himself for a moment like this. Or maybe he knows that, just a few moments ago, he stepped over the line. Going from a man who could justify what he had done to a man who committed violent acts for no other reason than it was in his nature.

Or maybe he's banking on the fact that he knows I won't pull the trigger.

After all, I'm the good guy. The man in the white hat. For all my flaws, I have always tried to do the right thing. The only men I ever killed, I killed them because they were threatening my life and the lives of those closest to me.

At least in part.

So what is my justification here?

Why do I have to kill David Burns? Why is there no other choice?

Seven years ago I shot a man. Knocked him off his feet. Watched him die in the mud and the

2

rain, his blood diluting as it sopped through his shirt.

He deserved to die.

Same as the old man does now.

Yes. David Burns deserves to die.

I can end all the years of misery and heartache. To gain some kind of justice for all the people caught in his sick pool of self-indulgence and greed.

So do it.

Do it, you fuck.

Do it!

My finger finds the trigger.

He remains on his knees with his head bowed. 'I didn't kill Ernie. I didn't kill your fiancée. I didn't bring you to this. But if it makes you feel better . . .' Is he taunting me?

I had it all back. Had it together. Was moving on. Rebuilding my fucking life. And what was it that pulled me back down? Back to this?

David Bloody Burns.

Always David Burns.

The albatross around my fucking neck.

I see it, now.

Everything leads here.

High above the city. Surrounded by the dead and dying. Blood diluting in the rain.

Making this choice.

All I have to do is squeeze.

All I have to do is squeeze. And it ends.

Tonight.

In blood.

It's so easy.

He lifts his head. Maybe thinking that I won't do it. That I won't kill him.

3

He thinks he knows me. He has manipulated me every step of the way.

So here, now, I have to make a choice.

No hesitation.

Trust your instincts, McNee.

He starts to smile.

I squeeze.

One

Three days earlier

Findo broke down the door, roared on through. Shouting. 'Rise and shine, fucking cuntybaws!'

I followed behind. Cricket bat in hand. Mask over my face. Full on frightener. Yelling at the top of my lungs. The adrenaline pumped. Didn't make me feel good.

But this is what we were paid to do. Who we were paid to be. The heavies. The bad guys. 'The welcome wagon,' as the old man had said.

At the time, I had tried not to let my distaste show. This was my life, now. This was who I had sold my soul to become. And even if it was a lie on my part, I found it hard to justify what I did in the name of my cover. Knowing that others were doing worse, that the old man was treating me with kid gloves.

This kind of job made me sick to my gut. Going against everything I had once been. Making a mockery of the copper I used to be, the investigator I had become. Knowing what I was doing, the reasons I was doing it. I wanted to walk away every time, throw my hands in the air and say, 'Fuck you.' But I couldn't do that. I was in too deep. I had no choice but to pretend like everything was OK.

Pass the bloody Oscar.

Or maybe not, because the real reason I felt sick was that I knew some part of me was enjoying this. How else could I have convinced the old man of my apparent change of heart? Of my willingness to give up everything I had to work with him?

Some skinny prick with a bad case of bedhead poked his head out from one of the rooms. Findo went for him with the pipe. The others pushed past me. There were five of us, but me and Findo were the go-to-guys. The ones in charge. We said how fast, how hard, how far.

Findo always wanted to push farther.

I was the cautious one.

For oh-so-many reasons.

One of the reasons the old man decided to pair us up. He liked the idea of opposites working together, figuring there was some kind of balance in that.

I winced beneath my mask. My breath bounced back against me under the thick wool. My chin was developing a rash. I was being stifled. Wanted to push up the fabric, take in a gasp of pure air; a drowning man breaking the surface of the ocean. But I repressed the instinct, focussed on the task at hand.

I pushed past the rammie that was breaking out around me, made for the room at the end of the hall. Kicked at the door. Got nothing but a sore leg. Went for the shoulder. Got it open, let the momentum pull me inside.

The fat man roared at me as I stumbled into the room. He was naked from the waist up, hairy like an orangutan that hadn't got the hang of shaving. His jowls wobbled as he screamed. He had been trying to do up his belt, had given up on that when I blundered into the room with my size tens. He ran for me, head down. I figured I knew how a matador might feel. Every footstep from the fat man measured on the Richter scale.

I sidestepped, and he carried on past me. His momentum slammed him into the wall. I swear, the whole building shook.

I swung the bat and caught him in the kidneys before he could straighten up.

All the same, he stayed standing. Turned. And grinned. His mass had absorbed the impact like it was little more than a swat from a rolled up tea towel.

I didn't pause. Swung back the other way, curving up, cracking the side of his face. He screamed something I couldn't understand and went down on his knees.

I allowed myself a little grin. Said, 'This is your eviction notice.' Worrying that maybe I was getting a little method about all of this. Too much into character.

'Fuck you.' The accent was strong, but the words were clear. 'Fuck you, you Scottish fucking prick. Cunt!'

First thing you should learn when you need a second language: how to curse.

Lard-boy had it down good.

Findo came through, finished what I had started by smacking the fuck's skull with his pipe. The big guy went down. Still breathing, though.

Thank Christ.

7

Some things you have to do. Others, you'd rather not find out whether you can.

'Real shitehole, this place,' Findo said. 'Fuck knows why the old man gives a crap.'

He gave a crap because the Hungarians were stepping on his territory. Listen to his rants, he sounded more and more like the *Daily Mail* for criminals; talking all the time about how these foreigners were coming in, taking territory that belonged to men like him. What were they thinking, the old man would ask, opening up our borders like this? We were letting in a tidal wave of greedy, morally bankrupt arseholes.

Aye, like I didn't see the irony in his words. But I never said anything. Keeping the old man sweet was my job description. He had to trust me. Want to keep me close. That was the deal. That was the end game.

That was why I was breaking into apparently empty warehouses and cracking the skulls of fat Hungarians while trying to figure out how to stop my psychopathic colleague from actually killing anyone.

'Anybody else at home?' Findo yelled. 'This is your fucking wake up call!'

Findo Gaske. The psychopath in question.

Hard man. Gym freak. Clean-living thug. Way he told it, he used to have a bit of a habit, jacked it in when he realized you were better off as a supplier rather than a user. He'd always been a big guy, and when he went to David Burns to ask for employment, what he got was a gig smashing heads. As the old man said, 'Some pricks, you just look at them and you know what their skills are.' Turned out Findo was better than even the old man expected. If you get a job like that, it helps to enjoy it.

His capacity for violence was one of the reasons Findo had more responsibility than I did. Just because the old man liked me didn't mean he wasn't aware of my moral compass. Hell, we'd fought about it more than enough in the past. He was probably still trying to figure out just how I had readjusted my morality that I would come to him looking for work.

Findo had been working for Burns for a couple of years. Earned his way into a position of trust. Authority within the organization. That big head had a few brain cells working. He was more than just muscle. He knew when to deal out the pain and when to hold back. But he always preferred it when holding back was the second option.

It was no wonder he didn't take to me. Findo had worked to get where he was. I had waltzed in on the old man's say-so.

'Hear that?'

I listened.

'Bit heavy for rats, aye?'

He had a point.

The noise came from a back room. As we walked through, the bare boards creaked beneath our booted feet. I'd taken to wearing steel toes for gigs like this. Bit of advice that Findo gave me. You never knew what you were going to find, and if you had to give out a kicking, you wanted it to hurt.

Also, wearing steel toes meant less broken

foot-bones if the thing you were kicking happened to hurt back.

Working an undercover gig, you don't want any cause for suspicion. What you want is to blend in. And sometimes that means doing things you found distasteful. Like maybe giving a guy a kicking when he didn't deserve it. Or beating down some naked fat fuck with a cricket bat. And pretending like you're enjoying it.

Two

'You understand?'

'Aye.'

'I know you feel like I manoeuvred you into this . . . but believe me, you were the only logical choice. And I needed someone who already had connections to the old man. Someone I could drop in fast. Someone David Burns would be pre-disposed to trust. He always treated you like a wayward son. You've admitted that yourself.'

'Care to tell me why you needed someone so fast?'

Sandy Griggs steepled his long fingers, looked at me over them. His red hair was tousled. Not out of any sense of style, but because he had other things on his mind than how he looked. There was shabby-chic and then there was simply shabby. Accounted for the wrinkled shirt and jacket he was wearing, too.

We were in my offices at 1 Courthouse Square.

Eight months before Findo Gaske beat the shit out of a fat Hungarian man, using a lead pipe.

I had a knot in my stomach. In hindsight, bad as it felt, it probably wasn't tight enough. But I wasn't stupid enough to not be afraid of what was coming. Says a lot that agreeing to go undercover with the old man seemed the least dangerous of my options.

Or maybe I just told myself that.

Griggs had the look of a man trying not to tell the truth. Word around Tayside Constabulary had always been that he was the kind of man you didn't want on the other side of the table during a round of poker. Could have fooled me. He wore his anxiety like a suit. Better pressed than the one he actually had on.

'This time next year,' he said, 'there will be no SCDEA. You've heard, haven't you?' Of course I'd heard. Alex Salmond, Scotland's First Minister, was disbanding old policing structures, introducing a new, unified Scottish police force. The old divisions would be gone. No more Fife. No more Tayside. No more Lothian. The force would be as one. Police Scotland. The shiny new face of twenty-first-century Scottish law enforcement. As well as the old divisions collapsing into obsolescence, so were newer and more modern institutions like the SCDEA. The Agency would be enveloped into Police Scotland, but no one seemed sure of the details.

'You're running out of time.'

'Maybe we'll still be operational in a year's time. Same game, different initials. You know what bureaucracies can be like. But I'd rather

11

not take any chances. Besides, this operation against the old man has been running for close to ten years, now. I'm not the first man to head it. The SCDEA didn't start it. There were others before this even began. But we're running on empty, now. Despite everything we know about David Burns, we've never been able to bring him in. Never had enough to satisfy the Procurator Fiscal's office.'

'Which is why you need me. Why you needed Ernie Bright'

He nodded.

I understood why Griggs had been so heavy-handed in his pursuit. David Burns was fascinated by me, in his own way. Time and again the aging hard man had made overtures about how I should join his outfit. Painting himself not as a crook, but as a man of the people. The police, in his mind, were little more than automatons following a party line. Men like Burns, on the other hand, understood the complex needs of the population and were therefore entitled to do whatever was right for the people.

Regular fucking Robin Hood. Or at least that's how he always wanted me to see him.

Burns's view of me as a sympathetic soul meant that, if I pressed the matter, I was perfectly placed to get close to the old man, to uncover his secrets.

Which was why Griggs figured I'd make the perfect honey trap. Thankfully, without the sex.

By the time of this particular meeting, I had already made an overture to Burns. Not in the way that Griggs had expected, and not in a way I'd ever go into detail about. That was fine by

12

Griggs, just as long as I delivered what he needed. We both understood that sometimes undercover work could involve undertaking actions that were morally uncertain.

What I'd done for the old man was deliver him a killer. A man who had murdered children, including the son of Burns's neighbour. Burns killed the twisted fuck, weighted the corpse and tossed it deep into the Tay, where he could rot at the bottom of the river for all anyone cared.

I had watched the execution. It had been an initiation, I suppose.

The first step in our new acquaintance.

A first step from which there was no turning back.

'Are you willing to do what the old man tells you? He will test you.'

He had already tested me. When the old man killed a child murderer in front of me, it was as much a test of my reaction as it was the legitimate passing of a sentence against a man who had transgressed Burns's personal moral code.

But David Burns was not the type to trust easily. I would be expected to do more than just passively observe acts of violence. I would be expected to get my hands dirty. Whether Burns accepted my personal moral code or not, he would expect me to follow his orders. Obey his rules.

As part of our arrangement, Griggs assured me that as long as I stayed within certain parameters of behaviour, he would be able to give me a clean slate when the old man was brought in.

I wanted to ask: is this what he offered Ernie Bright?

Did anyone ensure that he had understood the risks? That he knew there was a possibility he could wind up dead in an abandoned warehouse, his chest torn apart by a shotgun blast, his life and career in ruins?

But I didn't say anything like that. Because by then, there was nothing left to say. The chance to back out was long gone.

I was in deep.

All I could do was try and keep my head above water.

Three

Eight months later. The same room as the unconscious fat man.

Findo nodded to a cracked door on our left. Ajar. The wood warped just enough to prevent it closing all the way.

I shrugged but didn't say anything. Findo's hearing was clearly better than mine. He was still young. I was a curmudgeonly thirty-eight, although parts of my body felt closer to sixty after all the beatings I'd taken down the years.

Findo hefted his lead piping, and kicked in the door. In his head, he was probably Arnie or any number of eighties action movie heroes. I'd been in Findo's flat, seen the posters he had framed: *Cobra, Commando, Red Dawn, Lethal Weapon*.

'Awright, you pricks! Listen up! This is . . . holy shit! McNee! Get your fucking arse in here!'

14

Concern in his voice. Not something I'd heard before. Usually, Findo was swagger and bravado. No compassion. No empathy for other human beings. But there was a catch in his voice that didn't sound right. Like he didn't know the proper way to react.

I walked into the room just behind him. Small. Same bare floors we'd seen everywhere else. What light there was cracking through grime encrusted windows. Flat pack bunk beds, shoddily assembled, adorned with ratty quilts. Clothes on the floor. Takeout cartons here and there, some still half full. The smell of rotting food mixed with distinctly human odours.

Bodies moved. Hesitant. Uncertain.

Three girls, maybe in their early twenties. Dark hair, big eyes, skinny frames. The kind of skinny you could count their ribs. They were in various states of undress, covering themselves up, hiding behind the frames of the bunk beds for whatever protection they could find.

Slowly, Findo lowered the piping he was still holding high over his head. Look closely at his eyes, you could see the cogs turning behind them. Listen hard enough, you could hear them, too. He was a certain kind of smart, but when it came to things outside his experience, he could be slow on the uptake.

'What the fuck is this? McNee?'

I ignored his question, walked forward, holding my hands out to show I didn't mean any harm. One of the girls, the one closest to me, watched me with eyes that were too scared to blink. She was tense, and when I came close, she moved

15

her head back. Her thin body twisted like a cat recoiling from a threat. But she didn't move from where she was. The hesitancy was countered by the fact that I wasn't presenting a threat. I wasn't yelling, screaming, raising my fists. I crouched down, took her hands in mine. Keeping the grip soft. She could move away if she wanted to.

But she didn't.

Her eyes locked with mine. I wanted to weep when I looked into them.

'It's OK,' I said. 'We won't hurt you.'

She shuddered. Bowed her head. Let go of my hands and collapsed on to the floor.

I looked up.

The other girls continued to stare at me. Saying nothing. Their faces blank. No emotion showing.

Were they afraid?

Or simply unable to process what was happening?

Four

'Call the police. Call the fucking police. Let them handle it.'

'You're sure?'

'That's what the old man says. Just make sure you get the fuck out of there, OK?'

'Aye,' I said. 'Right.' Not really listening.

I was on the phone, still crouched next to the girl I'd first approached. She was still hunched in on herself. Afraid that I would suddenly turn

16

on her. She didn't know what I was saying into the phone. She had barely understood what I had said to her. Her English was confined to rote pleasantries, words she'd been taught to say. No doubt to please men who maybe looked like me and Findo.

The voice on the other end of the line belonged to Michael Malone. Burns's mouthpiece. The cops called him The Lieutenant. Because that's what he was. The one who did the grunt work, made sure everything ran smooth. If the police wanted, they could have put Malone away decades earlier. But since everyone knew that he was simply the public face and not the man giving orders, the idea was deemed pointless. The exercise had always been about putting away David Burns, not the men below him. Cut off the head, you kill the snake. Old-fashioned thinking, but effective. And even if someone had the bright idea of trying to break Michael, it wouldn't work. He was too loyal. Like anyone who got that close to Burns, he worshipped the old man with the fervour of the religious fanatic.

'Make the call,' Malone said. 'Then scarper. Leave the girls. Just fucking go. Old man's say so, yeah?'

Fine. I hung up. Looked at the girls. They were shivering under blankets. I'd managed to persuade them to come out from where they were hiding, got Findo to make sure they were covered and in as good health as could be expected. They were underfed and clearly abused, but for the most part seemed in no immediate danger.

Having done his good deed, Findo stood by

the window, looking outside. As though he couldn't cope with what we'd found, just wanted it all to go away. He'd got over the shock, started thinking about the implications of our discovery. Couldn't handle them. This was not the kind of situation he was comfortable with.

He liked the simplicity of violence. Knowing that his choices were as simple as to kick arse or have your arse kicked. This kind of situation just didn't belong in his world.

But he understood what was happening. He knew things about how the world worked, just preferred to ignore them. But now he couldn't, not when it was happening right in front of his eyes.

There were more girls than we had first seen. Six in total. All underfed, half-dressed, terrified of the men who had burst into the tiny room they'd been calling home. They'd probably been here for months. Compared to the way they'd been brought into the country, I suppose it seemed like five-star luxury.

There were marks on the girls, too.

Didn't need to be a forensic investigator to figure what had happened to them.

I dialled the emergency line from my mobile, asked for the police.

'Can I have your name, sir?'

'John MacClane.' Figured she might not get that I was lying. Whatever. I couldn't leave my real details, much as I wanted to. The girls were a complication we didn't need. And you can't break cover because of the overwhelming urge to act like a white knight.

I hung up. 'We need to leave.'

'What about them?' Findo finally speaking.

'The police aren't dumb. I know. I was one of them, remember? They'll work out there's a human rights violation operating out of this address. Might take them a few minutes, like.'

'A what? Oh. Aye.'

'We'll have legged it by the time they get here, Fin. Don't worry.'

'Right.'

'Old man's orders.'

'Direct?'

'Through Malone, but he talked to the old man.'

'OK,' Findo said. He turned to face the girls. 'We're leaving now. Me and my friend. But it's OK. Everything's going to be OK. You understand?' He spoke slowly, thinking that might help them understand what he was saying.

But of course, they didn't understand. Just looked at him with a mix of fear and incomprehension. Wasn't just about understanding English. With someone like Fin, you needed a PhD in the Dundonian accent.

'Do you understand? *Comprende?*' Each word shouted in an attempt at comprehensibility.

'Fin, that's French.' Or at least an attempt. But I kept that last thought to myself.

'European, though? They're European, right? They have to speak French. It's like the fucking law over there.'

I shook my head. Said, 'Come on. We need to get out of here.'

As we left, Findo turned and said, 'You never saw us. *Merci Beaucoup.*' Even if they could

19

speak French, chances were, given Findo's accent, they'd still have been left without a clue.

Five

When I walked into the Gateside Pub that evening, Susan was already seated near the rear wall, nursing what looked like a simple Coke. The main bar was small, the tables intimate. Quiet, but then it was a Tuesday evening, and traffic out this way had been light. It was the kind of pub where you were either a local, or you'd had to make a special journey.

The girl behind the bar said, 'Looking for food?'

'Meeting someone,' I said, and nodded to Susan. 'But, sure, we'll be eating.'

'She didn't seem so sure.'

I took the menus and went over to Susan. The girl poured a pint while I sat down. Susan said, 'The food's good. I just didn't know . . .'

'No, we don't really see enough of each other these days, aye? Good to have an excuse.'

She smiled at that. But it was a sad kind of smile, and made me sorry that I'd said anything.

She said, 'I used to come out here with Mum and Dad. My aunt lived in the village.'

'Nice wee place.'

The girl from behind the bar brought my drink, said, as she placed it on the table, 'Friendliest village in Scotland.'

'That a fact?'

'We got an award and everything.'

Gateside's a small village maybe thirty or forty minutes' drive after crossing the bridge to Fife. There's not much there, except the pub and a garage that specializes in Minis. It's nestled beneath the Lomond hills, feels out of the way, the kind of village – maybe its closer to a hamlet – where you can imagine everyone knows your name. A real community. The point of meeting here was that it was isolated from the city; no one knew me or Susan or our connection. Unless maybe they recognized Susan from when she visited her aunt. But then that wouldn't mean anything to anyone.

'Ready to order?'

'Give us a minute.'

As I studied the menu, Susan said, 'So tell me what happened?'

'Today? We were supposed to be putting the frighteners on some morons cutting into the old man's business.'

'What kind of business?'

'The usual. Drugs. Cutting into the old man's territory. The girls were a surprise. No one was expecting that. Not the old man, anyway.'

'No?'

'Say what you like about him, he has principles. His prostitutes are always of legal age. And as to people smuggling, well, only the lowest kind of animals would stoop to that.'

'You sound like you admire him.'

'Don't. Just because he has principles doesn't mean I agree with them.'

21

She looked up from her menu. 'I'm sorry.' And she meant it, too.

'It's tough enough,' I said.

'Of course.'

We sat in silence for a while. Studied our menus. Every time we met, there was the same awkwardness. There had been a time we were close, but the events of the last few years had served to distance us from each other. Events that might have brought other people closer together had only pushed us apart.

I often wondered if it was more my fault than hers. There were things that should have been said or done that never were.

I said, 'So what now? What's the grand plan from my masters at the SCDEA?'

'No official word, but I figure . . . we keep going as we were. This doesn't change anything. I mean, what does it achieve? In the bigger picture?' I could see from the way she refused to look at me that she hated herself for sweeping what I'd discovered under the carpet. In the old days, these kind of things would have been impor-tant. To both of us. What did it say that we were unwilling to step up?

'I don't . . . I don't know,' I said. 'But Burns thought these guys were small time drugs dealers. This is bigger than that. I don't know . . . maybe we can turn this to our advantage.'

Hypocrisy, thy name is McNee.

'Maybe. You're the man on the inside.'

'You put me there.'

She didn't say anything. Except, 'So, you ready to order?' Like we'd just been discussing perfectly ordinary business. The girl from the bar was standing behind us. How much had she heard? How much did she give a shite about?

I looked up. Not ready to order. Barely having glanced at the menu. But I made a stab anyway, ordering the first thing my eyes fell on. 'Sure, the pheasant.'

'Me, too,' Susan said.

When we were alone again, she said, quietly, 'I'm sorry how things worked out.'

'Sure,' I said. 'So am I.'

Six

There was a message waiting on my other mobile as I walked to the car. The night air was cool, the wind gently caressing my cheeks. Inside the pub, the heating had been too high, and to exit to the gentle cool of the night and the quiet of country roads felt like walking into another world.

My mobile screen lit up bright in the dark. The message was from the old man. An address. The intent clear. No clue as to why he wanted to meet, but then I wasn't supposed to care about such things. The rule was this: he said jump, you didn't even ask how high.

I drove back via country roads, passing the Bein Inn, a hidden music venue on a back road that had been a booming business for decades. I wound past small gulleys before hitting the road

23

to Perth, merging on to the motorway and rocketing on towards Dundee, approaching from the west.

Coming from the Perth direction, you get a sense of what the city used to be. The skyline is still peppered with the high rises that used to dominate, although these have slowly diminished as the council tries to erase the mistakes of sixties and seventies town planning. There's a sense that the urban landscape is creeping up on the countryside; the city slowly expanding out and into the world, spreading its grey among the green.

It's an odd sight if you know the city, because Dundee has great whacking expanses of greenery through its structure. The city has adapted around the green rather than absorbing it.

I slipped through on to the Kingsway – the ring road that runs round the city – and headed round to the North as though making my way to Aberdeen. I hit an industrial estate, slowed, and pulled into the near empty mass of old buildings and concrete car parks.

The building I wanted was the only one with a vehicle parked outside; a black Merc with 2012 licence plates. One of the old man's indulgences.

The warehouse was, ostensibly, a storage facility for Burns Construction. Kept clean with regular security checks carried out by the big man himself. Walls have ears, so the saying goes. So do telephones, chairs, windows and floorboards. When he asked for a cleaning crew, he meant people to check for signs of the cops. The rats. Pest control had a different meaning in his world.

I walked into the building, was met by a heavy I'd never seen before. Young lad, looking ready to tear off that tie and loosen that collar. The old man was a stickler for appearance, insisted that people who worked for him looked at their best. He was a conservative crook; the kind of man who pined for the good old days when kids showed respect for their elders. The good old days where people turned a blind eye to criminals who were just looking to earn a living.

The thug gave me the traditional pat down. I said, 'You know who I am?' meaning it like a joke and not getting a response never mind any hint of a smile. Maybe the joke wasn't that good. Maybe the kid had heard it before. Maybe.

When he was done, he gestured for me to walk up to the mezzanine level, where I could see the office lights were on. I got lightheaded as my fingers touched the cold steel of the bannister.

My mentor had died in a warehouse like this.

I always used to wonder if he had any knowledge of his impending death.

Burns didn't stand as I entered the lean-to office at the end of the gangway. He merely smiled and gestured at me to close the door. No warmth in his smile. He wanted me to know that he wasn't going to make this easy on me.

Of course not.

Had he already talked to Findo?

There was a bottle of Grouse on the desk, maybe a quarter gone. Two deep bottomed glasses beside it. He poured himself a belt, then waved the bottle at me. I refused. I'd been drinking less than usual since this assignment started. Best to keep my wits about me. I'd never been much of a drinker to start with, so it didn't seem too out of character. But there were moments – and this was one of them – where all I wanted to do was neck down something strong, lose myself a little while, take the edge off the seemingly constant adrenaline.

'So tell me what happened.'

I did. Taking my time. Keeping the details clear. Not getting carried away with embellishments. Stick as close to the truth as possible, you don't have to remember too many lies. The old man listened, sipping at his whisky, sometimes nodding.

When I was done, he said, 'That's what Fin says, too. Except he was the calm one in his version.'

'That right?'

'Oh, he wanted to impress me. Lad like that, doesn't look good he didn't know what to do. But your version sounds about right. That's all I needed.'

I remembered the importance of keeping witnesses separate when interviewing them regarding certain incidents. The stories didn't need to line up exactly. People's retelling of the same event can differ on details. It's human nature. Anything too exact is as suspicious as a wild divergence.

I wondered what else Findo had expanded on in his telling. And what I had consciously or unconsciously added to my own narrative.

'Did you know? About the girls, I mean?' After all, he had sent us there. And everyone who worked for him knew that sometimes the old man lied.

He shook his head. 'No. Far as I knew, this bunch of pricks were small time, trying to muscle in on the powder trail. Shaking down loyal customers, offering cut price product.'

'At cut price quality?'

At least that gave him an excuse for what passed for a smile. 'Aye, what can I say? The drug connoisseur has gone the way of the dodo. Now you could give them powdered dog worming tablets, say it was finest Bolivian, and they'd say thank you. If the price was right.' He belted back the last of his dram. 'Standards, lad. Standards have gone out the fucking window, you ask me.'

It was hard to disagree.

'There have always been . . . grey areas . . . in my business. Always. Some things that give you pause. Some schemes where you have to wonder whether what the coppers say about you isn't true. But this shite,' he said. 'This shite you and the boy Findo came across . . . I don't like it. Never have. Men who trade in women like that . . . they're scum, lad.'

Burns wasn't above prostitution. Most of the local pimps, and some of the independents who plied their trade on the wrong streets, kicked a cut back up to the old man's outfit. Which worked out fine, most of the time. The girls under his protection were safe. Anyone who stepped out of line soon knew about it. He was the caring criminal. All part of his redeeming self-image, you see. He had standards. An ethical sense.

27

There were lines. Even for men like Burns. And this was one of them.

'The girls are fine,' he said, as though I'd just asked the question. Maybe to reinforce the fact that I hadn't. 'Thank God.' He still had his own lines into Tayside, a few cops on his payroll who kept him up to speed on affairs. One of the reasons I had been approached by an outside agency, at least according to Griggs. As far as anyone was aware, Burns didn't have anyone on the inside at the SCDEA. Much as he kept trying.

'Yeah?'

He looked at me for a moment, and I had to wonder if he knew or suspected my secret. The old man had been perfectly aware of Griggs's overtures to me, but when I proved myself to him, he'd never mentioned the DI's name again.

All the same, there had to be some suspicion.

In deep as I was, I still wasn't deep enough. Not for Griggs, anyway.

What was it between Griggs and the old man? Back when all this started, I'd got the idea that they somehow knew each other. Which made sense. Griggs was a former Dundee cop, the old man had been around nearly forever. There had to be some connection.

But I always got the sense that Griggs was taking his investigation into the old man far more personally than even an embittered ex-cop had any right to. Like maybe there was some deeper reasoning to his need to put David Burns behind bars.

Or perhaps I was just getting paranoid. Given the events of the past few years, it was surprising I wasn't seeing conspiracies in every shadow.

Burns said, 'They're fine. The girls. So I hear. Shaken up. Scared. Malnourished. But in no immediate danger.'

'Except from deportation.'

He smiled. 'Tell you who I'd deport, the bastards who forced them here.'

'I thought you said these guys were a small time crew.'

'Who graduated too fast. Strange, isn't it? And there's the other thing . . . these fuckers were supposed to be strictly local. Both you and Fin said about the fat guy . . .'

'The accent.'

'European.'

'Hungarian.'

That got me a raised eyebrow. 'Oh, you're an expert, now?'

I shook my head. 'Just . . . back when I was in uniform, I used to do some community work round where a lot of Hungarians had moved to. You learn to recognize things. Like accents.'

'And the girls were Hungarian, too?'

'I think so. Wish I'd paid more attention to the language.'

'They come here, they should speak English.'

'I don't know that these girls really had much chance for a distance learning course.'

There was silence for a moment. The old man and I looked at each other. The only thing worse than accidentally revealing my intent in getting close would be showing disrespect.

Had I blown everything with just one sarcastic remark?

'Maybe you have a point,' he said. 'The girls

aren't to blame. It's just . . . fuck!' He poured another belt. Then straight into the second glass, which he held out to me, his face telling me there was no way I could refuse this one.

'There's something else,' I said, taking the glass, nursing it. 'Something you're holding back. From me and Fin. You didn't know about the girls. But we've hit three houses in the last month. Always small time. The same crew, I'm guessing. Someone you want to send a message to. But this is the first time we've found something on this scale. To traffic people like that, it takes a tight network and some very big connections. And I don't think someone could be that well connected without you being aware of their activities.'

'No flies on you.'

'I'm an investigator.'

'Aye, and tell me, how's that working out for you?'

It was a low blow. My official status with the Association of British Investigators was on hold. Pending potential criminal charges.

That had been Griggs's doing, of course. His way of getting me closer to Burns, of convincing the old man that I was no angel despite what I tried to make out.

When this was over, I didn't know what was going to happen. The ABI was strict on matters concerning membership ethics, and even if I'd believed myself innocent before the charges were brought forward, I'd done things since hooking up with Burns that I couldn't undo. Even if Griggs had those quashed, there would still be a stain

30

on my professional character that would be hard to wash out.

'Tell me,' I said.

He took a deep breath. 'A few years back, this young prick came to me. Balls on him, you wouldn't believe. But the brains of a fucking mental midget. Said he was looking to expand his little business, that he had good contacts in Eastern Europe, could move some decent gear.'

'And?'

'And I had some associates check him out. You know how I work, McNee. All business. No fucking with people. No making arrangements with people I don't believe can follow through on their promises. You deal with my people, you know what you'll get.'

Fucked up or dead, in my experience. But I wasn't about to say that.

'Little prick had a record. Nothing wrong with that. I believe in second chances. But it was a record for assault. On his own sister, you believe that?'

The word 'assault' can bring a variety of associations. But from the way Burns said it, I got the impression that this young prick wasn't just about using his fists.

'That why you didn't work with him?'

'Never make an uninformed decision.' The tone of his voice like he was Lord Sugar passing on business advice to one of his apprentices. 'Some of my own lads vouched for him. Said he was changed. That they knew about him from word on the street. So I took a few deliveries. Discovered he was keeping me sweet and some of my own men even sweeter.'

31

Meaning he was shifting some of his product direct through dealers, not kicking the full vig back to Burns. Letting the dealers keep a little themselves as an incentive.

Dangerous game. For everyone involved.

'What happened?'

'Someone dropped the wee prick in it. Anonymous, of course. He did his time in Perth prison. And I figured maybe that would give time to think on his approach to life. A bit of solitude can be good for the soul.'

'And now?'

'You're the investigator. The ex-copper. The man who unearths people's secrets. You tell me.'

'He's out.'

Burns didn't say anything.

'And someone's trying to muscle in on your territory. Probably using supplies from Eastern Europe. Which makes you think it's the same prick.'

'You always get there eventually.'

He offered me a second belt. I refused. He poured a third for himself. Hard to tell how many he'd had already. He was one of those drinkers who didn't really change when they got drunk. Probably had a tolerance after all these years. Men of a certain generation have a tolerance that no one else can understand. 'So you and the boy Fin have been doing my legwork. That's what I've been hiding: that I've got a bona fide reason for hitting these particular operations. I really didn't want the wee prick muscling in. Figured someone gives him a skelp, he might finally get the message and move on.'

'But now . . .?'

'He needs more than just a skelp. The girls . . . I won't stand for that kind of shite. I'm a family man, McNee.'

Aye, if that family's the Manson family.

'Of course,' I said.

'His name's Nairn. The prick, I mean. Craig Nairn.'

'Craig Nairn.'

'You were always good at finding people, McNee. Why don't you find this cunt?'

'And then?'

'Have a quiet word in his ear.'

'That's all?'

'What kind of a man do you think I am?'

Talk about your loaded questions.

I stood up. 'I'll do what I can.'

'There's a bonus in this one.'

I shook my head. 'No bonus.'

'No?'

'Like you said, this is about the girls.'

'Good lad,' Burns said. He smiled. 'Good lad.'

Seven

Back at my flat, I tried to make a start on finding Nairn. But I was exhausted, ready to give up before I even started. Even firing up the PC, all I did was stare at the homepage and think about what I could type into Google, none of the possibilities exciting any action in my fingers.

33

So I threw myself on the couch, channel surfed until I dozed off. Woke around nine and moved to the bedroom, where I collapsed on top of the covers and passed out completely.

I don't remember dreaming, but when I woke again about half-three, I was drenched in sweat and tangled in the covers. Like I'd been fighting them in my sleep.

I had told the old man I'd find Craig Nairn.

And what then?

The two of them have a nice wee chat, sort things amicably?

Aye. Right.

Griggs had told me he would clear me of any criminal charges, ensure that I was allowed to do what was needed without fear of reprisal. But there were limits. Not just for what he could clear me of, but for what I could stomach doing.

What worried me most was the idea that I could stomach it. That I felt something of the old man's righteous anger. I wanted to find Craig Nairn. Punch his face into hamburger meat. Use my bare hands. Make it hurt.

We'd both said it, the old man and I: *This was for the girls.*

I used to think there was a line separated me from men like Burns, but the more I pretended to work with him, the more uncertain I became that I was pretending.

Were our intentions so far apart? Were we so different, as I had always claimed?

I had slept only a few hours, but I couldn't force myself to relax enough to pass out once again. I hit the bedside light, walked through to the living and turned the TV on for company.

Twenty-Four-Hour News Cycle. Even the presenter looking bored, aware that at this hour most people were drunk and tuned to Babestation or wired on coffee and economic anxiety, trying to solve the pay-per-play quizzes on some of the higher up channels for a quick cash-hit.

I just needed the sound of a human voice. Something about the BBC news was comforting. There was a house style that was almost reassuring.

I pulled out the hidden laptop from where it was taped behind the sofa. Let it whirr into life. Took me two tries to get the password, the mix of capitals, numbers and symbols dancing about in my groggy, sleep-deprived brain.

I opened files. Read details. Reaffirmed my moral superiority. Reminded myself why I was doing this. Whose side I was really on.

David Burns. Born in one of the failed social experiments popularly referred to as 'schemes'. Brought up hard, despite being the middle son of a hard-grafting family. Saw his friends fall to drugs. Learned from their failures. Not that drugs were bad, but that the right man could make a good profit shifting them. He saw other's weaknesses and realized there was a living to be made exploiting them. But he wasn't dumb enough to simply dive in feet first. Burns had a natural understanding for the order of power, knew he couldn't just make it to the top in a single bound. The only people who did that were jammie bastards or psychotic bawbags. More usually both. And while some people would have called the old man psychotic, the truth was far more complex than that. So Burns played the long game. Ingratiated himself with local gangs. Worked his way up from thug to trusted confidant to man tipped for the top. Became privy to the city's other political system. Learned that the real world and the underworld weren't so separate as people believed.

He played a long game. And played it well. Just the right mix of business savvy and inescapable violence. When power came his way, he consolidated his grip on criminal activities while simultaneously cultivating a more respectable public persona. He was a businessman. That was his line. A businessman. And who could blame him for a rough past given his upbringing?

It was a necessary fiction. A reimagining of his early years. Not just for the good of his legal status, but for himself. Burns began to believe his own lies.

He was a family man. That much was true. But it was only his own family that he was concerned for. No thought was ever given to the families of those whose assaults and deaths he ordered, and occasionally participated in. But that didn't matter. He became an expert at separating his actions and his beliefs, somehow able to balance what he did with what he claimed to believe.

I had to wonder if he would look at the reports of his own crimes and recognize the truth in them, or if the moral outrage that would explode from his aging but still deadly frame would be genuine and absolute. Had his own lies now become more real to him than the truth?

When I was young, my gran was the one who told me about heaven and hell. She was a believer, of course. In the fine traditions of the kirk and the Church. She told me once that even if you behaved like a decent person on the outside, presented a fine public figure to all those you encountered, then God would still know the truth. Would still judge you and find you wanting. Because, inside, you can't disguise your own guilt. She said that God knows the truth about us because we know the truth. We can't escape it. We can tell all the lies we want and become so good at telling them that we can fake belief in our own delusions. But when it comes to Judgement Day, none of that will matter, because we cannot hide the truth inside ourselves. Sooner or later, as the song says, God's gonna cut us down.

I wonder whether God would be able see the truth inside Burns. It often felt as though the old man had performed a miracle of ethical alchemy. For him, now, the truth was his own righteousness. His sheer strength of belief trumped any independent evidence. He would genuinely believe that his accusers were the ones deluding themselves.

I read his biographical notes over and over. My eyes watered from the glare of the laptop screen. A needle started digging just above the bridge of my nose.

Maybe it was stress. Brought on not by focussing on backlit screens or tiny text, but by David Burns.

Were we really so close? Could we finally bring him down?

Did I want to bring him down? This killer and self-proclaimed 'family man'?

Family, as I had found over the last few years, was not just flesh and blood, but those you surrounded yourself with. If you were close to Burns, he treated you well. I had been aware of that for a long time. During Ernie's attempts to gain favour with the old man, Burns had treated his contemporary with grace and good will. Made him part of the family. Bonhomie and generosity had been the orders of the day. Enough that I came to believe Ernie really had fallen for the old thug's schtick.

I had misunderstood. Seen only what Ernie needed me – and the old man – to see in that moment. For over two years I would believe that the man who had been my mentor was in reality a corrupt and rotten cop who had fallen for the charms of a psychopath. Ernie would die before I learned the truth. Before I followed down the same path.

Had Ernie been this conflicted? This uncertain about what he was doing?

Burns's solution to the people traffickers was swift and brutal. Outside the law. Immediate. Designed to satiate the natural feelings of revenge and injustice that accompanied the crimes we had witnessed.

To take down a man like Craig Nairn by the letter of the law, the authorities would follow a slow set of precisely choreographed procedures. Unable to strike until the situation was perfect. The same procedural behemoth that allowed men like Burns to feel they were one step ahead of the law. They could move nimbly, where the law lumbered.

What Burns offered felt like real justice. Quick. Decisive. Driven by emotion. It was what we all wanted deep down beneath our thin layers of civilized behaviour.

Because it was easy.

I had gained the old man's trust by bringing him a sacrificial lamb. A child killer who had fixed up an innocent man for his own crimes. One of the sickest men I had ever encountered. His attempts to explain his crimes as a kind of illness had made me feel the old rage rise in me again. I had wanted him dead. It was what monsters like him deserved. When I watched Burns slit the child killer's throat, I did so with the kind of cruel satisfaction I imagine crowds used to experience when viewing public executions.

The guilt came later. The shame.

How could I say I was so different from Burns when I had that kind of anger inside me?

How could I know that I shouldn't be turning myself in as well, when this operation was finished?

Eight

Findo called at my flat the next morning around seven. When I answered the door, he looked surprised. 'You're up?'

39

'So are you.'

'Had to force myself out the pit. Fucking hate mornings.' On closer inspection, there were black lines under his eyes. His lines were cut deep into his face. Had been since his early twenties. Old face, young body. And even though he was a gym freak, he hadn't yet given in to full-on male vanity. Moisturiser was for 'wankers', apparently. I wondered what he'd look like in twenty years. If he lived that long.

'Yet here you are,' I said,

'You going to piss me about?'

'What do you want?'

'How about you start by letting me in?'

I relented. He came in, went to the living room, looked about. Something of the dog in the way he moved. The way that a canine will sniff around an unfamiliar room to make sure there's no danger waiting. It was the first time I'd let him over the threshold.

'The fuck is it with you and the Spartan life? And what the fuck, man? No fucking new films here? Jesus, haven't you seen *Avatar*? Anything past 1995? Fucksakes!'

I was in the kitchen, getting him coffee. Black, two sugars. I didn't shout back a reply, just prepared the coffee and then went through. I said, 'Most films after 1995 are shit.' I didn't add: especially the ones by James Cameron.

'And music?'

'Same thing.'

'Yeah?'

'A few exceptions.'

'The old dinosaurs still kicking on?' he said,

40

sniffing round the CD rack like a cat with the scent of litter. 'Nick fucking Cave, man? Jesus. What you want is some fucking beats, man. Like, oom-cha-oom-cha, know what I mean?'

Unfortunately, I did. He controlled his car's radio like a prison guard controlled his keychain. Afraid it might be contaminated by anything they wouldn't play at Liquid on a packed Saturday night. You knew when Findo was coming down the street. Hell, you knew when he was three streets away. The ground shook like Godzilla was stomping his way drunkenly down the Marketgait.

The human beatbox turned away from the CDs. 'Besides, no one has discs, now. All digital, man.'

I was glad he hadn't noticed the vinyl. 'Guess I'm behind the times.'

'Gotta get with it. Can't be left behind. Dinosaurs, man, you know what happened to them?'

'They went extinct.'

'See what I'm saying?'

'Sure.'

He looked at the bookcase. 'Like this shite. Fucking books, man. Even the nerdy bookworms know you don't read paper any more. Get the Kindle on your mobile, whatever, take this shite with you wherever you go.'

'I like the covers.'

He picked a book off the shelf. Leered, and said, 'Can see why.' The cover of John Lange's Zero Cool looked back at me; the girl on the beach with the gun. Lurid in the best pulp fashion. Of course, Findo didn't see the history of pulp fiction in the hand-painted cover. He saw the girl

41

with legs up to here. Thank God he didn't pick up Christa Faust's *Money Shot*. The title alone might have given him a heart attack.

'OK,' I said. 'Pleasantries over. You've seen the cave. You know I'm an out of touch old man. So what is it you actually want?'

'Reckon we start the way we mean to go on. I got a lead on some of Craig Nairn's places. He runs a couple bars, like. We go in and give the bartenders a wee message, aye?'

I shrugged. 'We're the early birds.'

He looked at me like I was mad.

'Catching the worm?'

His brow creased. I tried again.

'When you were a kid, you went fishing, wanted worms for the hook?'

He shook his head. Should have figured Findo wouldn't have the patience for fishing. I used to try all the time down at the Dichty as a kid. But the pickings were slim, of course. Took me a few years and the first signs of maturity to realize if you wanted fish you went for deep water. By then, of course, I'd lost interest in the idea of fishing at all. Mostly because I'd discovered girls. Even if girls hadn't discovered me.

'Earthworms only come up to the surface when it's raining. Attracted by the vibrations of the rain hitting the ground. You wanted them for bait, you'd stomp around and wait for them to come up before grabbing them. Like a bird.'

Still not getting it.

'By hitting Nairn's places, we're stomping the ground so he'll show himself.'

42

'Right. Whatever.' He slugged back the coffee.
'Let's get a move on if we're going then.'
'Fine. We're taking my car, though.'
'Aye?'
'I'm going to teach you about music.'
'Aw, man! Jesus fuck!'

Nine

Alabama 3 took us to Lochee high street. Pulling in at the side of the road, I experienced the old sense of unease that used to accompany beat walks through the area. Lochee has a reputation – deserved or not – for poverty and danger. The sense that it is somehow separate from the rest of the city adds to the degree of unease. Especially if you look like you don't belong.

Looking up the main street towards the library, which was housed in a grand old building as you left Lochee and headed back towards the town, I saw some guys in cheap jeans and horizontal-striped polo shirts lounging around. Smoking cigarettes. Generally wasting time. One of them had a bag at his feet. The kind of bag that would clink if you kicked it. They turned to look our way, maybe wondering who we were and what we wanted. When they saw Findo, they quit looking. Guess his face was known round these parts. Or it was ugly enough that suddenly the guys figured whatever we wanted was none of their business.

Findo didn't pay attention to them. He had that kind of confidence. Maybe they had attuned to that. No sooner was Findo out the car, than he was walking down in the opposite direction, towards the Crow and Claw. He walked with purpose. Strong strides. Arms swinging. Anyone got in his way, he'd have walked right over them.

The Crow used to be owned by a guy called Big Ian Machie, before he toppled over from a heart attack at 58. Machie had been neutral in Dundee's turf wars, declared the Crow a free drinking ground for all. His one edict was that no one conducted official business on his premises. His rules were backed up by a cricket bat. And one hell of a swing. Since his passing, the pub had fallen into the hands of a guy named Coleman. On the way over, between his grudging appreciations of Alabama 3, Fin told me that Coleman was one of Nairn's front men. 'Fuck knows where he's getting the money to buy off a guy like that, but that's the word on the street.'

Coleman was an older guy with a hearty laugh and a slap on the back for everyone. But he had always been one for dancing to someone else's tune. One of life's natural followers. For the most part, the old man had little interest in Lochee. Gaining a foothold there had always been hard for him, and he finally reached the decision that it was simply easier to leave the place alone. But since Coleman had fallen in with Nairn, what had been one of the quietest pubs in the city soon became a nightmare call out for any copper with a radio and a patrol car. I heard through the grapevine that nowadays, uniforms would play coin toss or scissors-paper-stone to decide who answered Crow call outs. In the old days, they'd just pop in their heads for a wee pint, rubbing shoulders with the kind of pricks they'd arrest if they saw them out there on the high street. Now, they were no longer welcome. In the brave new world of twenty-first-century Dundee, there were no longer neutral spaces.

As we walked down the street, Findo said, 'Those fucks weren't so bad.' Talking about the music again. Like he'd been considering it a long time, finally reached a decision.

'Glad you liked 'em.'

'What's with the religion though?'

The Church of Elvis the Divine? Someone needed to get Findo a dictionary so he could understand satire.

We hammered on the doors of the Crow. I used the old police knock. That attention-grabbing hammering that you pick up after a few years on the beat.

We waited.

After maybe a minute, a voice said, 'Piss off. Don't start serving til eleven.'

'Open the door,' Findo shouted back.

'Go fuck yourself.'

'You know who we work for?'

'Could work for the Good Lord Himself and I wouldn't open the fucking door. Not that this time. Jesus Christ himself could be out there dying of thirst, and I wouldn't spare a glass of Buckie.'

'How about David Burns?'

'Fucksakes!'

45

The door opened in double quick time. Coleman sweated through his shirt. The effort of turning keys had clearly been enough to threaten a major cardiac incident. 'Why the fuck didn't you say so?'

'You had to ask?' Findo said. 'When we knock like that?'

We pushed past Coleman, into the pub.

Coleman locked the door behind us. 'So, what can I do for your man, then? I mean, has to be something special for him to send two fine fellows all the way over to Lochee.' As he turned back to face us, he wiped the back of his hand across his forehead. The sweat dripped.

'Can the shite,' Findo said. 'Or I'll can it for you.'

I propped myself against the bar. Coleman's eyes were on me the whole time, even though Findo was the one taking the lead.

Findo knew what he was doing. Playing it like a pro. In another world, he could have been interrogating prisoners of war on behalf of the Government. Would have made the whole war on terror a lot shorter with men like Findo around.

The bar itself was basic. Wooden floors, heavy oak bar, tables and chairs that could have come out of a church hall. In the days of Big Ian Machie, the place had style, although whether that was a good or bad thing was a matter of some debate. But under the new ownership, the Crow had gone back to basics. Pints in plastic tumblers. No food served in case customers decided to use the forks for more than just

46

stabbing at the blackened meat of their burgers. Aye, it was that kind of place.

Coleman said, 'Look, we don't have any argument with David Burns. He doesn't give a fuck about us. He's said so . . .'

'Your boss has an argument with him.'

'I own this place. I am the boss. And I . . .'

'Don't shit a shitter.'

Coleman had forgotten about me now. His focus was on Findo. He'd figured who he needed to be afraid of. Forget me. I was the silent partner. Findo was the Voice of God.

Coleman looked ready to make a run – or at least a stumble – for the door. Not that he'd get far. I figured on a stitch before he even reached the back office. Coleman was nothing, really, in the grand scheme. Just a front. A name on the licence. A wee man at the bottom of a very big and very greasy pole. Old, out of touch, out of place.

And now, out of time.

Findo hopped behind the bar, grabbed one of the whisky bottles from the back wall, unplugged it, took a swig. 'Fuck, that's good.' He waved the bottle in my direction.

'Too early for me,' I said.

He waved it at Coleman. 'No. No, its fine.'

'Your loss.'

Findo poured the liquid on top of the bar. I stepped back. Kept watching. Thinking this was all a bluff. Findo was a mental, but I figured even he had his limits.

Coleman was frozen. Even if he wasn't scared before, he was terrified now. His face was grey.

The sweat rivuleted down his face like Niagara Falls.

Findo said, 'Tell that arsehole Nairn that we're on to him. If he wants a fucking war, we'll give him one. It's not too late, like. Not too late at all. So he can consider this a warning, aye?' He casually reached into his jacket and pulled out a silver zippo. Flicked the lid. Grinned. Probably saw the move in a movie somewhere. I wondered who he thought he was at this moment in time. Which particular badass he was channelling. Someone from the eighties, no doubt.

'Oh, come on, man,' Coleman said, voice raising an octave in desperation. 'Insurance is a bitch. You want me to talk to Craig, that's grand. Fuck, I'll get him to get in touch with the old man if that's what you want. I don't know what he's done, but he's not an eejit. It's nothing worth blowing out of . . . oh, come on!' Findo had flicked the flame into life.

I forced myself to keep still. Keep my face in neutral. Observe.

'Tell him we're serious,' Findo said. Flicked that naked flame against the bar.

Coleman lumbered to the door.

Findo looked at me.

I looked at the bar. The flames whipped over the surface. I figured when they hit the booze behind the bar, we'd be in trouble then.

Coleman was trying to undo the locks. Fumbling each one. Fat fingers drenched with sweat, slipping against the cool metal of keys and Yale locks.

Findo was cool as a cucumber, still by the bar.

48

'Come on, man,' he said to Coleman. 'We'll roast alive in here.'

'Fuck you!'

'Aye, OK, so think of it like a steam room. You're sweating off the pounds. Jesus, be nothing left of you after a few minutes. Big fat bag of skin, maybe.'

'Fuck you!'

The last lock. Coleman fell out on to the street.

Findo strolled. I followed. Forced myself to keep pace. Like I was in control. Like this was all in a day's work.

On the street, Findo walked to Coleman, grabbed him by the collar, spun him round and kneed him in the groin. As the big man went down, Findo leaned into him and whispered something I couldn't hear.

As we walked back up to the car, Findo said, 'That's how you stamp out the worm, man.'

Ten

Back at the flat I took a long shower. Scrubbed hard. Every inch of my body.

How much longer?

How much more?

I had more than enough evidence to take to court, but it wasn't enough for Griggs. Maybe nothing would be. The SCDEA agent wanted to take down Burns hard. Nail the old bastard for every criminal act he had ever committed. And more, besides. I got the feeling that, if he could, Griggs would have fitted up Burns for the death of Princess Di.

The question was: why?

I knew dedicated cops. I knew obsessed cops. Men and women who would do whatever it took to arrest the bad guys. They took cases personally, allowed themselves to empathize with victims, as though they had personally been violated by the perpetrators.

But Griggs's dedication verged on the creep level of a stalker.

There was something else going on. I'd seen hints over the last few months, but it was more intuition than anything concrete: whatever was between Griggs and Burns, it was clearly personal. And it went back a long way.

As I came out of the shower, the buzzer screeched. I picked up the handset by the door and said, 'Yes?' figuring it was Findo again. Probably another little mission. The old man's obsession with Nairn was nearly as bad as Griggs's obsession with the old man himself.

Burns hadn't been properly challenged on his home turf in a long time. Maybe he was worried about the idea of new blood on the block. Particularly new blood he couldn't respect.

'Open up, McNee.' OK, so it wasn't Findo after all. Aye, but it was the last person I wanted to see.

DS Kellen.

It had been bad enough when I was a straight up investigator, getting hassle from DI Lindsay. But at least me and the former DI had history.

Maybe even understood each other to a degree. Since he got invalided behind a desk we'd even come to a kind of mutual understanding, although it would be hard to characterize us as friends.

But now that he was no longer a threat, I had Kellen on my case. She was a recent transfer from Lothian and Borders, the kind of DS who wanted to prove herself. Ambition ran through her veins. She had decided I was how she would make her mark. The way she saw it, I was the one who got away. A murderer who cheated the system. Back when she first transferred in, a little bird dropped a crumb on her desk implying that I had perverted the course of justice. The little bird had been Griggs. It had been his way of making sure that I towed the line and took his offer seriously. He claimed it was all part of a scheme to make my approaching the old man seem more natural. But he set the ball rolling long before I agreed to work with him.

The evidence had been quashed as soon as I signed up to Griggs's scheme. Some behind-the-scenes politicking. But rather than dowsing her interest, it only made Kellen more determined to uncover some deeper level of corruption to my case. She was certain I was using old contacts to bypass the law.

She believed in truth.

Reminded me a little of the person I used to be.

I had the door open when she came up to the third floor. She looked at me and said, 'Just getting up? No wonder the business closed.'

'It's temporary,' I said. The offices still belonged

51

to me, and my secretary was still on pay. The business was being temporarily backed by David Burns. Something that made me sick to my stomach. But both Griggs and I figured it was a necessary evil if we were to retain the old man's trust.

'Until you can convince the Association of British Investigators to let you back into the fold?'

Kellen went into the kitchen. The coffee was percolating. She grabbed a mug without asking. Making a statement. She had the power. She had the control.

She was right, of course.

'You been in Lochee the past few days?'

I didn't say anything.

'Just there was a small case of a pub burning down. I'm sure you remember the Crow and Claw.'

'I remember Big Ian Machie.'

'Before my time.'

'You wouldn't have liked him.'

'Oh?'

'Morally ambiguous. Couldn't categorize which side of the law he was on. Good man, though.'

'Everyone's got a side, McNee. Moral ambiguity is an excuse for those who don't have the stomach for the law.'

'Liberals?'

'The only party I vote for is the one that's tough on crime.'

'Nice to know you have a flexible attitude to policing.'

'I'm not without compassion.'

'Good to hear.'

'When it's deserved.'

'Did you just come round here to piss me about?'

She shook her head. 'Witness statements place you and Findo Gaske on Lochee High Street prior to the incident.'

'Oh?'

'Oh, indeed. Look, I don't know what happened to you, McNee. By all accounts you were a good copper and maybe even a decent investigator. But whatever happened, whatever it is that Burns holds over you . . . there's no excuse. No excuse for what you've become. You will pay the price.'

'You came round to threaten me?'

'To ask you to do the right thing.'

'What if there is no right thing?'

'There always is.'

'That's the world, then? Black and white? Good and evil?'

'Yes. Shades of grey are for people who prefer excuses. You do a bad thing, there's no excuse in the world for it.'

'I'll bear that in mind.'

'I know you killed a man in cold blood,' she said. 'Maybe that could be spun as excusable, given the circumstances.' She bit at her lower lip as though thinking about what she'd just said. 'Self-defence? Justifiable force? Your life was threatened, of course. But there's the matter of the extra weapon. The one you say belonged to the man you murdered. You and I both know that weapon didn't belong to either man. You deliberately concealed a deadly weapon. You took it with you. You intended to use it on these men.'

'There was no pre-meditation. The dead man

53

dropped a second, concealed weapon. I took the opportunity to defend myself.'

'Tell yourself that. You were heading this way all along, McNee. Everything that's happened to people around you, everything that happens to you, it's all your own fault. You brought this shitestorm down on your own head.'

I'd already reached that conclusion long ago. Made my peace with it.

'Tell me what happened with your fiancé. They never did catch her killer, did they?'

Maybe it was supposed to blindside me. The man who ran us off the road had never been found. For years I had to live with the fact that I had survived and Elaine had died. That our last words to each other had been terrible, hurtful.

I used to blame myself. Blame the argument.

When the truth was that sometimes the world just throws bad things in your path. And you have to deal with them.

I said, 'No, they never did find him. And you should be careful, throwing around accusations like that.'

'No one's accusing anyone of anything.'

'Aye. Right.'

'All I'm saying is that they closed the case, but I'm keeping my eye on you. Your new friends are going to send you down, McNee. Sooner or later we all get what we deserve.'

'We're done?'

'I'm done.'

When she was gone, I took the mug she'd been using and threw it against the wall. Watched it shatter.

Eleven

The fire made the news. STV covering the blaze on the lunchtime bulletins. Live updates from the scene. Either it was a slow news day or someone was using the blaze to gain maximum publicity.

I could imagine who.

'The fire at the pub has been linked to local gang activity. DS Amanda Kellen of Tayside Police has stated that the Crow and Claw was a known site of local gang activity and had been under police surveillance for some time.'

Cut to Kellen on the steps of FHQ. Proclaiming to the assembled. I shook my head, cut her off before she had a chance to start. She wouldn't mention my name. Her talk would be as vague as she could manage. A good soundbite. She, like so many before her, knew how to use the media by giving them nothing, but taking as much as she could from them.

I grabbed my mobile, stabbed in a number. Waited a few rings before the gruff voice on the other end said, 'What the fuck d'you want?'

DI George Lindsay. My former nemesis. Now a desk jockey and hating every minute of it. As he said himself, 'who the fuck ever locked up the bastard bad guys by pecking away at a bloody keyboard?'

Our relationship was friendlier than in the past.

Which mostly meant that he would talk to me without shouting too loud. At least that meant we could dispense with opening small talk, get right down to business. I reckon he preferred it that way. 'Kellen talk to you?'

'Of course.'

'And?'

'And I told her what a prick like you does is none of my bastarding business. Gave up trying to understand you a long fucking time ago.'

'Thanks for the vote of confidence.'

'What, we're friends, now?'

'Maybe.'

'Like shite, McNee. I gave you a chance after that business with Ernie. I stood up for you when you sent the Assistant Chief Constable down on corruption charges. But these days . . . I don't know what the fuck you've got stuffed in that skull instead of brains . . . but whatever the fuck it is, it's making you dumber than one of those bastard *X Factor* contestants.'

'At least you think I can sing.'

'The bollocks who get booted off in two minutes.'

'Right.'

'I can't tell you who to hang around with, son. I can't tell you when you're being an arsehole.'

'Could have fooled me.'

'Aye, laugh it up. Do the smartarse thing. See if I give a shite. But you're fucking it up. Big time. Just like your pal, Ernie Bright.'

They'd respected each other, Lindsay and Ernie. Despite their differences. For him to take the man's name in vain like that was a kick in the bollocks. Didn't matter how angry he was at me, I knew it was serious when he brought Ernie into the mix.

I hung up. No goodbye. No smart-aleck last remark. Just cleared the line.

I took deep breaths. My head was light, and there was a nauseous feeling in my gut. My hands were shaking. The world bent into the distance. It was an old sensation. As a teenager, I would take panic attacks. Over the years, they had vanished. But then a few years ago, I'd felt the beginnings of those old, helpless sensations reasserting themselves. I'd buried them for a while, but it was like they couldn't help reminding me that they were in there somewhere, waiting for me to let my guard down.

I took slow, steady breaths, focussed on them as best I could. Thought about my pulse, let it slow. Picturing the pumping blood as it slowed in my veins. A form of meditation. Nothing I'd been taught formally. Just a coping method. Thinking about nothing except my own physical state. Ignoring the rest of the world.

Finally, my breathing slowed again. The world snapped back into place. I closed my eyes, took a few more slow and steady breaths. When I was ready, I went through to the living room, sat down in the armchair that faced the front window and looked out at the cold-grey sky. Remembered how Ernie always used to tell me that despite the man's attitude, George Lindsay was the one truly honest cop you'd ever meet. He was brusque, angry, rude, hated everyone equally. But in some ways that made him more of a believer in equality than the most liberal man you could meet. And, importantly, he genuinely believed in innocent until proven guilty. He believed in the system.

'You can trust him.'

I never used to believe it. Lindsay and I had run-ins on a regular basis while I was in uniform. Culminating in the day I broke his nose before finally walking off the force. To my mind he had been a bully-boy arsehole. A relic of the old days of policing. And he never did anything to convince me otherwise. He didn't think he had to. Until the day Ernie Bright died. Until the day he decided that rather than fight me, we could work together.

Working with me nearly killed Lindsay. Got him attacked by a corrupt cop and left in a coma. But it made me understand what he was willing to sacrifice in the name of Truth.

So what happened to make our relationship slide so far backwards? Why was he returning to the old ways?

It wasn't just being back on the force.

Secrets.

Lies.

I wanted to tell him. To tell someone.

But I couldn't.

What's the old saying? Damned if you do, damned if you don't?

Sometimes there's nothing like a cliché for getting straight to the point.

Twelve

'How it works is easy,' Findo said. 'You go in the garden, walk round to the rear window and whistle. Like this.' He demonstrated. 'They drop the stash. You're done.'

It was a neat system. You paid in advance, you went to the meeting spot, gave the signal. The product technically never changed hands. Anyone arrested you, you said you found it lying around. Didn't belong to anyone. No, sir. No one.

It was a small time racket. But clever enough. Nairn was building his customer base. We were here to make a dent in it. We'd already hit a legitimate interest. Now we were showing him that nothing he had was safe.

So how did Burns plan to take Nairn off the street for good? Did we break his business? Or did we break him?

It was the kind of question I didn't really want to answer.

Burns knew that there were rules to our new-found relationship. I didn't deal. I didn't kill. When I told him, he nodded like he understood. And maybe he did. If I'd been overly enthusiastic about the murkier areas of his business, he'd have known something was wrong. As things were, I was behaving exactly as expected.

'But you'll rough someone up?'

'If they deserve it.'

'Tell me what deserving is?' As if he didn't know. He'd seen the kind of men I was willing to drop in the deep end. He knew where my moral compass pointed.

That hadn't been an act. Much as I might try to pretend it was.

Fin got out the car. I followed. Fin had the cricket bat he'd taken from the Crow. He was grinning like a maniac. Some guys get off on strip clubs. Some on adrenaline sports. Some on all kinds of weird sexual shite. But Fin liked violence. I remembered how he was in the warehouse. How, for him, it hadn't been about the job or even, in the end, about the girls. It had been about hurting people. In an odd kind of way, there was something pure about his attitude. With Findo Gaske, at least you knew what you were getting. No wonder Burns trusted him so much. The lad was easy to read. And loyal, too. You'd rather have him with you than against you.

We walked round the side of the building. Fin sent me on ahead. The scouting party. The canary down the pit.

The building was condemned, now. Built in the sixties, it had served its purpose and then quickly become a blight on the cityscape. No one really wanted to live here, and no one wanted to buy it. So it was abandoned. Weeds cracked through the paving stones that ran the exterior, and forced their way into the brickwork of the building. Glass cracked beneath my boots. Dead soldiers. Abandoned works. I pushed long branches out of my way.

I reached the back of the building. Whistled.

Would they realize I was little more than a distraction?

Ten seconds.

Twenty.

A plastic Tesco's bag dropped by my feet. Plopped from one of the second floor windows. I picked it up, looked inside. 'The fuck is this?'

No answer.

'The fuck is this?' Just in case they didn't hear me the first time. 'This is fucking short, man. Fucking! Short!' Making for outrage. Not exactly Oscar material, but enough to get a response.

'Get to shite, man! That's the bag.' The voice muffled from inside the allegedly abandoned building.

'Like yer maw's arse is this the bag. I want to talk to someone.'

'No fucking deal, man. Get on your bike!'

'Piss off! I talk to someone or . . .'

'Or what?'

'Or I'm fucking coming back with petrol and matches.' For good measure: 'I know my fucking rights!'

There was silence above. Maybe they were having a debate about whether I posed a serious threat. Whether I was even serious. I waited.

Then: 'Back door.'

Maybe they planned to teach me a lesson. Maybe they really were going to work out a refund or exchange. It didn't matter. I walked further round the building. Fin saw me, winked from where he was hiding behind the overgrown, sad bushes that lined the edges of the property. I didn't do anything, just stood in front of the

61

door. It looked heavy, paint faded, porthole glass at eye level shattered.

I waited.

The door opened. Two kids in shellsuits and peaked Burberry caps came out. Thought they were gangsters, had the cheap jewellery on their neck to prove it. They were pale, skin pitted with bad acne and eyes sunk into their heads. They blinked in the daylight. Skinny-malinky vampires robbed of their primal threat. One of them sneered at me and tipped his head. 'The fuck's your problem?' Oh yeah, he thought his middle name was Danger.

I stepped back.

They stepped out. Into the open.

Findo came at them from the side. No sound. No battlecry. No warning.

The bat caught the first kid – the one with the sneer – under the chin, snapping his head back. He didn't say anything. No noise. Just went down. The second kid did a skipping dance back into the hall. Didn't even have time to try and close the door before Findo was in, swinging the bat up and between the poor bastard's bandy wee legs.

I tried not to wince in sympathy.

We were in. Up the stairs. Behind us, the kids groaned and rolled and moaned. They weren't getting up anytime soon. We climbed single file, the hall too small to allow us side by side. Not that it mattered. I was following in Findo's wake. A small boat in the wake of a larger vessel. A pilot fish behind a whale.

Two more on the stairs. Findo smacked the first

62

one over the balcony. Only one floor, but once we were done here, I was calling an ambulance. The second took a glancing blow and folded. Findo stepped over him. But the blow didn't take the wee nyaff completely out of the game, and he tried to get back up. I stomped on his chest, leaned over, grabbed his fringe and smacked the back of his head against the stairs. He didn't move after that.

Later, I'd be concerned for him. There and then, I just needed to keep things simple. The direct route.

We made it into the supply room. Two more in there. Dressed in darker colours. One with a cap, the other with greasy hair combed forward and flat against his skull. The one with the cap dived behind one of the tables where the stashes sat waiting and emerged with a gun. He was shaking, fumbling as he tried to hold it correctly.

Not like in the movies, then.

Findo said, 'Fuck this,' and chucked the bat like it was a spear. It hit the poor bastard square in the forehead, and he dropped the weapon. The gun went off, the explosion echoing round the small room. The sound had a physical presence. My ears popped with the noise, and I hunched in on myself. When the noise cleared, became little more than a background hum, I checked myself just in case. No sign the bullet had hit me. I'd seen men shot before. I'd shot a man before. Didn't fancy the idea of a bullet ripping through my flesh.

I looked at the guy with the bad haircut. He

was on the ground. Hand at his side, jaw dropped, catching flies. He coughed twice. Said, '. . . the fuck?' and lifted the hand he had pressed against his side. Stained dark red with blood. He started to breathe fast, then flopped back. Passing out. Shock and blood loss.

Maybe he'd live. Hard to tell. But with prompt medical attention, I figured there was a good chance.

Findo was bending down. Came back up with the gun. No hesitation the way he held it. No doubt. The wee prick with the hat had been frightened of the gun. Probably never actually fired the thing before, just showed off to his mates, waved it around in folks' faces and expected them to fear him.

Gun runs on the force had always been bad news. Like a nuclear bomb had been found in the city. The kind of call that made adrenaline spike. They were unexpected. Unknown. Dozens of officers at a gun scene. Specially trained firearms officers flanking normal uniforms, everyone keeping their distance, everyone terrified.

I'd been at the centre of a gun raid once, as a civilian. The officers who stormed the room had been wide-eyed with restrained fear. This was Scotland, not South Central LA. We have firearm issues, but rarely do they cause a real problem.

Findo said, 'D'you feel lucky, punk?' He hoisted the gun, pointed it at the guy with the cap.

'Come on, man,' I said. 'This isn't . . .'

'Shut the fuck up!' He turned his attention back

to the punk with the hat. 'Well? Do ya?' Clint Eastwood with a Charleston twang.

The kid backed off. 'Come on, man. This isn't . . .'

'You know the kind of cunt you work for?'

'I don't know, man. Just come here, do the work . . . like, better than on the dole, know what I'm—'

'Do you know the kind of man you work for?'

'I—'

Findo pulled the trigger. The kid's head jerked back. His body twisted. Blood arced.

I watched. Like it was a movie. A computer game. A TV show. Something separated from the world that I knew and accepted as real.

I didn't feel anything. Not at first.

Not for a few moments that were more like hours.

Findo turned away. Dropped the gun on to the hard wooden floor. And smiled.

I ran for him, head down. Roared so loud my throat scraped like a cheese-grater.

Thirteen

Findo's breath slammed out of his body, right as my shoulder slammed into his midriff. I wrapped my arm round his waist, the momentum carrying us both back and over the table. The bags broke along with the table and we crashed on to the ground. Powder exploded. Wood cracked and splintered.

65

I rolled off Findo. Tried not to breathe in the powder that had exploded into the air. My body ached. My muscles stretched to snapping point. Bruises threatened to form across my abdomen and upper body following the impact. I waited a few moments and then used the wall to clamber back on to my feet. My movements were stiff and slow. I looked down, saw I had wound up next to the prick with the cap, the one who now had a hole in his face. I swallowed. Tasted copper and vomit.

Findo got to his feet. Slowly. Maybe feeling the same pain I was. But he was confused. His face twisted with a lack of comprehension. 'The fuck, man?'

'There was no need for that. Jesus, you didn't have to kill anyone!'

'Fucksakes, you really are a Bubbly Bairn, aren't you? I've been telling the old man you don't have the stomach for this. Every time, he says you're an asset. Aye, well, he'll soon know, eh?'

'We were here to fuck the operation. Not kill anyone.'

'Is that your line, then? Fucking think about it, pal. We sell drugs. Those drugs kill people. One way or another. What I did was fucking humane!'

'That's not what I'm talking about.'

'You sure?'

I ran at him again. He was ready this time. Sidestepped and locked me into a headlock. His thick forearms threatened to cut off my oxygen supply. My head swam in bubbles. He walked me round fast, got my feet off the floor and

66

threw me on top of the corpse with the hole in his face.

I got back up, fighting the urge to vomit. My legs felt light and useless beneath the leaden weight of my upper body. But I remained standing. I wiped the back of my hand across my face, certain I could feel blood there.

'You done?'

I wasn't done, but there was no point running at him again. I held up my hands. Findo laughed, stepped towards me. 'You'll learn, pal.' Like all was said and done. Forgive and forget. Like I was the kid here, the one with a lot to learn.

I took a deep breath. My legs felt more solid. My head clearer. I could think straight. I could step back, look at the situation and see what needed to be done.

When Findo was close enough, I grabbed his shoulders, hoisted my right knee into his balls. Hard. He let loose a loud breath and collapsed. I grabbed the back of his head, slammed his face against the side of the table. He didn't resist.

He collapsed.

I watched him for a moment. No movement other than his chest rising and falling. He was still alive, at least. Although in that moment, I could happily have killed him.

I staggered back, pulled my phone out my pocket. Swapped sims with the one hidden behind my driver's licence. Called Griggs. Figuring he might have a few ideas.

Fourteen

'So what happened?'

No sign of the old man. No, this was the kind of shite he stayed well away from. Instead I was dealing with Malone, the buffer between the old man and his less than legitimate businesses. Bald head, white goatee, tattoos on his arms he liked to show off with short sleeved T-shirts. Used to work as a bouncer at some of the rougher clubs during the eighties. Still looked like he could hold his own if he had to. Short, but tough. Not exactly a wee man complex, but more like he had compacted the muscles of a man twice his size. Had this thing about baring his teeth when he got impatient. Used to be that was the warning to anyone stepping out of line. So far, he'd resisted with me.

But only because he'd likely been told to go easy.

'What happened was we got caught up in a raid.'

'A raid?'

'Seriously. Findo, he didn't . . . I mean, he didn't fucking think. You know how he is. He was in the zone. Neither of us thought. But he was right in there, and then the cops and then . . .'

'And then?'

'And then I got the fuck out of there.' Like he had to ask.

We were in the backroom of a barbers near Dens Park. The owner had watched us walk through the front shop with his eyes narrowed. He didn't like us being here. But then he probably had no choice. Like so many people, through accident or design, he was clearly in debt to the old man. A gambler or a John, maybe. Didn't look like he had issues with drugs, anyway. The eyes were too clear. Just a normal man who made some stupid mistake.

But then isn't that the way with most folk who get dragged into the wrong side of the law? It's never so much a conscious decision as it is a perfect storm of circumstance: interior and exterior influences in perfect alignment.

Malone nodded. 'You used to be polis.'

'Aye, I did.' I was seated on a swivel chair. Even walking from the car across the road had been an effort. The fabric of my shirt had brushed against the bruises, lighting them up, reminding me of the punishment I was putting myself through.

'No favours?'

'Ask the old man if you like. I've been a pariah for a long time when it comes to Tayside's finest.'

'Stand up.' No emotion there. No hint he gave a toss about my explanations.

I did as he asked.

'Take off your shirt.'

'Not without dinner and flowers.' Didn't get a smile, so I pushed it. 'Even a movie would do.'

'Take it off.' Sounding bored. Humour not his thing.

I undid my shirt, took it off. Slipped off my

69

T-shirt, too. Gave him a pirouette that wouldn't trouble Wayne Sleep. 'Happy?'

Malone nodded his head down the way.

'Fucksakes.'

'You going to make this hard?'

'For you or me?'

Malone smiled. 'Guess.'

I undid my belt. Dropped the jeans. Held my hands high. 'Happy.'

'Can't be too careful.'

'No. You can't.'

No wires. No recording devices of any kind. That was the rule. Me and Griggs had gone back and forth on the idea, but even though I'd worked my way in close to Burns, the fact remained that the old man was a paranoid of the highest order. He regularly checked his closest friends for wire taps, hired cleaners for his home who were also trained in the art of surveillance detection. He wasn't just scared of the police. He was a target for far worse than men in uniform.

Malone seemed happy. Gave me a wink and then pulled out his mobile. Dialled in a number. Waited. 'He's here. He's clean.' Then, to me: 'Sit.'

I grabbed the swivel chair next to the desk.

Malone stood by the door. Like one of the Queen's Guard, I suspected he wouldn't have moved for anything.

I was struck by the scene. The man waiting in the room. The strong, silent type by the door. Put Malone in uniform, I could have been a suspect waiting for the lead detective to arrive.

You always keep suspects under observation.

70

You never know what they might try. I'd seen cases of suspects trying to strangle themselves with handcuffs, battering their heads off desks and walls, all in an attempt to avoid the inevitable. The confession. By the time they were in the room, they knew it was coming

Burns arrived about ten minutes later. During this whole time, neither Malone nor I said a word to each other. We understood the situation. Knew the roles we had to play.

When Burns entered, I stood up.

The old man said, 'Should I be worried?'

'Findo won't talk.' But I couldn't be sure that's what he meant.

'No, he won't. And you?'

'I'm here because I had the good sense to get out.'

'Aye, Findo always was impulsive.' Already speaking about him in the past tense. 'The idea of getting you two together was that you might have curbed his excesses.'

And, I supposed, he might have helped me find mine.

'But instead, McNee, you go and make him worse. What is it between the two of you? Always had you down as a people person.'

'I don't know.'

'He never trusted you.'

I nodded.

'Maybe he saw you as a threat.'

'Maybe.'

'The new golden boy.'

'Basic Freud.'

'Without the bit about shagging your mother.'

71

'Right.'

'That was a joke.'

I gave him a laugh. A dutiful one. He shook his head. My laugh wasn't enough. 'Sit, McNee. Sit down.' He rarely called me by name. Usually 'son' or 'lad'. Made me worried. Meant the situation was serious.

I did as he asked. No fooling around. His expression was taut. His eyes impossible to read. Was he angry at me? Or someone else?

Did it matter?

'I've already sent a solicitor down to the station. Fat Boy McArdle.'

Euan McArdle. Bane of every arresting officer's life. The kind of solicitor you turned to when you wanted sleazy, sweaty, crumpled amorality. He was going to end his days either rich, arrested or at the bottom of a ditch. Even money whatever way you looked at it.

'He talked to Findo yet?'

'They're playing with him just now. Delaying the inevitable. You know what they're like. Especially if they think they can get anything on the likes of me. But McCardle will get in the room with our boy.'

I nodded. Wondered if Burns could see the sweat on my forehead. An ocean of cold shivered through the pores in my skin, drenching me, dripping in my eyes.

But if the old man saw anything, he didn't react.

Which somehow made things worse.

'Think he's going to say something different to your story?'

How do you answer that?

'God knows.'

'Oh, He does, lad. He knows everything.'

Fifteen

Back at the flat. In the shower. Heat turned all the way up. Skin lobster red. The pain enough to keep me awake. Eyes closed. Colours dancing in the dark. The sluice slapping against my skin.

I was alive.

I could feel it. In the water. In the heat.

I was alive.

For now.

When I was finally done, I towelled vigorously. Skin softened, threatening to rip off beneath the thick material of the towel. It felt good. I felt good.

I was alive.

The idea percolated in my brain. An important thought. Something to be remembered.

The buzzer intruded. Insistent.

Kellen?

Not Findo.

The old man, then? Malone? Someone with a gun or a knife?

Schrodinger's hard man? You'd never know until you answered the call.

I answered, wrapped in the towel, still dripping water. If death was waiting, I wasn't meeting him with dignity.

'It's me.'

I buzzed her in.

Susan.

Memories.

Mistakes. Skin against skin. Whispered words. Broken promises. Secrets that tie people together as much as they tear them apart.

Susan and I had a complicated history.

We almost worked it out. A few years back, just before her father died, we almost got it right. But we had always been hanging by a thread, and the revelations in the wake of Ernie Bright's murder marked the beginning of the end for us.

She walked out. Went travelling. To 'find herself'.

No dramatics. No lingering resentments. No long building and simmering hatred. But things just went wrong. Wrong time. Wrong place. Wrong people.

I took it personally. Pretended I didn't.

And now she was back in my life. Sandy Griggs's lover. And his partner in the SCDEA. Both of them keeping it covert, knowing the kind of shitstorm that would come down on their heads if anyone found out.

Mind you, I had a feeling there was a lot that a man like Griggs kept hidden from his superiors.

'Why are you here?'

Susan walked through to the living room, sat down on the sofa and looked at me with eyes that hid their intentions. Her dark hair was cropped short, and she was dressed down in jeans and a heavy jumper. She looked tired. You could see it there, in and around her eyes. Bloodshot pupils. Dark patches that makeup couldn't quite disguise. Lack of sleep. You had to wonder why. Or maybe not.

'I know I shouldn't be here.'

'So why?'

'Tell me why you did that with Gaske? You put everything we've worked for in jeopardy.'

'He killed two men.'

'There are bigger—'

'Jesus!'

Silence between us. The Susan I knew would never have mentioned 'the bigger picture'. She'd have winced at the very idea. Had what happened to her been so bad that it destroyed her sense of right and wrong?

I remembered the death of the man who was responsible for her father's murder.

No one was ever sure who it was that burned down the storage container where he'd been tied up.

But I always had my suspicions.

We all do crazy things in grief. I should know.

I always wonder what would happen if I met the man who ran me off the road. So many years past. The car crash, and the death of my fiancée a memory, now. Sometimes it felt as though it had happened to someone else. Although I still retained the yearly ritual of visiting where she had died. As though I was afraid that to stop would mean losing her entirely. All the same, while the memory of the accident informed who I was, it no longer defined me in the way it once had.

All the same, I had to wonder.

What would I do if I met him? If I knew his name? His address?

Could I control myself?

Could I maintain the detachment I'd forced myself to build up over the years? Or would I discover the foundations were rotten? Useless, even before they were laid?

'There is a bigger picture, McNee.' Her voice was calm and steady. But just underneath that you could sense the hurt scratching away at the confidence, scrabbling to be heard. 'You know it. I know it. We wouldn't be here otherwise.'

'He killed two men.'

'He would have paid for it.'

'And so would I.'

'You've been paying for your imagined sins your whole life, McNee. I thought your dad was only a lapsed Catholic. Didn't figure he'd brought you up with the finer art of guilt.'

I went to the window, looked out at the street. The sky was getting dark. The threat of rain was in the air. An oncoming storm.

She said, 'We have to make sacrifices.'

'That you speaking? Or Griggs?'

'He's a good man.'

'Is he? Aye, well, he used to be. I know that much.'

'And now?'

'I'm not so sure. Being righteous is not the same as being right.'

I took the armchair. We looked at each other across the living room. Between us, you could have crossed time zones.

76

'He blackmailed me into this,' I said. 'Whatever way you look at it.'

'You're a stubborn man. Sometimes you need a little persuading.' A smile threatening at the edges of her lips. Something of the Susan I remembered. The woman I could have fallen in love with if I wasn't careful.

'You'd know better than most.'

She'd always been there for me. That was what still ate at my heart. I hadn't been there for her. She'd needed me when her father died, and what I did was take her grief and make it into my own. Shutting her out even more than I had before. If I hadn't done that, maybe things would have worked out different.

Maybe.

Maybe.

Life can become a series of regrets. If you let it. No one knows the shape of their world until they look back on what went before. What most of us see are paths not taken, choices never made. How we should have acted. We curse ourselves for being blind to those choices as though somehow we should have seen the consequences. Even though it would have been impossible at the time.

Are we fated to always make the choices we make?

Does it matter that we have the illusion of free will?

Are our lives determined by outside forces?

We are determined by biology, social standing, other people. We are never completely in control. We're barely able to keep a handle on our interior state, never mind what's happening around us.

Or is that merely an excuse?

Susan licked her lips. Swallowed. 'If we do this, we take down David Burns for good. We do what my dad always wanted. But we have to do it properly. We have to know he's not going to slither out from under us. You know that, right?'

'And what do we sacrifice for that? I can't allow more people to die.'

She seemed about to say something, but then she stood up. 'I don't know why . . .' She shook her head. 'I'm sorry. I shouldn't . . . I should . . .'

She walked to the door. I got up, ran to catch her. In the hall, I placed a hand on her shoulder. She turned round.

My breath caught.

I wanted to say something. Didn't know what. Didn't need to say it.

After, she sat on the edge of the bed. Didn't wrap herself in the sheets. Didn't grab her clothes. Just planted her feet on the floor, kept her back to me.

I said. 'I'm sorry.'

'Takes two, aye?'

'Guess so.'

'Always been a problem for us.'

'Guess so.'

More silence.

I got on my knees and shuffled across the mattress so I was beside her. Said, 'You and Griggs, still . . .?'

'Not for the last few months. You talked about righteousness. You and him, Steed, you're more alike than you realize. You're obsessives.'

'At the expense of everything else?'

'A modicum of self-awareness?' She let herself smile, and fell back on to the bed. 'Wonders never cease.'

'People can change,' I said. 'Sometimes they can grow.'

'It just takes a while.'

'Sure,' I said. I brushed hair from her temples. She was covered in a light sweat. Her breathing was a little ragged.

'Can we just lie here for a while?' she said. 'Not say anything.'

That was fine by me.

More than fine.

Sixteen

Susan left at ten that evening. I sat around for a while in the front room, lights off, thinking about what had happened, what it meant. If anything.

The same old mistake?

For both of us?

I thought about what she'd said about Griggs. Or rather what she hadn't said. As a copper, you soon realize that you can learn more about what a person has to say by their silences. It's the unsaid that matters. When you're always looking for the truth of a situation, it becomes an instinct. Even when you don't want to.

When I'd talked about Griggs blackmailing me, she'd shut the conversation down as best she could. Maybe feeling the same way.

She had said that me and Griggs were similar. I understood what she was talking about. Both of us were blinkered by a personal campaign that mattered more to us than procedure or due course. A campaign that mattered more to us than the people we knew, the people we loved. And the people who loved us.

My obsessions had taken me to dark places. I had killed a man because of them. Whether or not the gun belonged to him and whether or not he had threatened my life was immaterial.

The fact was that I had wanted to kill him. In that moment, when I pulled the trigger, I had done so with a clear head and an absolute purpose.

Taken a momentary pleasure in what I had done.

Because it was the only thing at that time that I thought would bring me peace.

The years since that night have all been about coming to terms with that moment. I have realized that it didn't give me what I wanted. That nothing I did could have brought me the satisfaction I had pursued. Nothing except time. And the grace of the universe.

I thought about all of this as the dark embraced me, broken only by the streetlights outside. I sat in the armchair in the front room, a poured but untouched Laphroaig on the coffee table. No TV. No radio. Just the sound of the city outside.

The bell rang about eleven, and I answered, my heart catching a moment like it used to when I was a teenager confronted with a girl I liked.

'You're awake, then.'

No such luck. There was no pretty girl on the other end of the intercom. The deep voice made my heart sink instead of sing. I swallowed my disappointment, buzzed the old man inside.

'Someone's got to Findo.'

'Aye?'

'He's not speaking to McArdle. He's not speaking to anyone. Which, in the plus column, means he's also not talking to the cops.'

'So why do you think someone's got to him?'

'I know the lad. His parents, too. I know when something's wrong. Fin would talk to McArdle. He knows the procedure. What he's supposed to do. So he's either already done something so fucking stupid he's afraid there's no way out. Or else he's not being allowed to talk to McArdle because the police are turning the wee fucker.'

We were in the kitchen. I'd poured a second Laphroaig for the old man. We sipped as we spoke.

Burns swirled his glass. 'You heard that about the bar in Edinburgh?' A non-sequitur, but maybe just thinking about what Fin might or might not have been saying was enough to give him the fear. The best way to deal with it was to change the subject. We were just two men having a nightcap.

'Which one?'

'The one . . . Christ, it was in those books . . .

81

the ones with the detective. Ribs, or whatever the fuck. The author made him drink in this bar . . . real place. Anyway, the story goes about how two wee American tourists went in and asked for the best whisky they had. Barman gives them two fine glasses. Fifteen-year-old single malt. Beautiful stuff. The Americans look at the drinks, then say, "Can we have ice with that?" Bartender takes away the glasses without a word and pours them down the sink. Turns back and says, "We'll not be wanting your custom, then."'

'That true?'

'Shite if I know, but it sounds good. Can't beat a good whisky. Wee bit of water to make it sing, and you're all set. To shite with ice, right?'

I raised my own glass. 'Right.' We clinked.

He didn't want to talk about Findo. Yet that was exactly why he showed up at my door. The old man was an expert in not speaking directly about things. Maybe that came with his line of work, his lifestyle. Or maybe it was a natural skill. Something inherent in his nature.

I said, 'He's not turned.'

'No?'

'One thing about Findo, he's loyal.'

'He didn't like you.'

'I posed a threat. Vouch for me all you like, he was still looking out for your best interests.'

The old man nodded.

'Took us a long time to get to where we are,' I said.

'And where are we?'

'At a mutual understanding.'

He nodded. 'I need you to do me a favour.'

'Right.'

'All this shite with Findo, it's going to draw attention. And I know you weren't happy with the situation. So I want you to do me a favour.'

'You already said.'

'Don't get cheeky, son.'

'Sorry.'

He sipped at his drink. 'My nephew's coming to town.'

'The one who owns the limo service?'

'That's the prick. And given the situation, I think he needs a new friend.'

'Close protection.'

'What?'

'That's the gig you're asking me to take on. Close protection. Bodyguarding.'

'Sounds melodramatic.'

'But accurate?'

He took another sip. 'It's not too hard. Keep an eye on him when he's out, that kind of thing. Make sure he gets left alone, if that's what he wants. But I doubt it. You could at least make sure he's talking with the right kind of people. Some folks, especially round here, they can get excited, you know?'

'Especially when you're the nephew of a local celebrity.'

He shook his head. 'A businessman, son.'

'And business is good.'

'Only as good as you make it.' He raised his glass. 'That's the only secret to success. Things are only as good as you make them.'

Trite bollocks. But the scary thing was, he believed what he was saying.

Seventeen

Robert Burns.

Aye, who said the old man's family didn't have culture running through their veins? Or a sense of humour?

Call him Rabbie, though, and all you'd get was a cold stare and the feeling he'd like to rip out your spine and smack you across the face with it.

He was in his late twenties, ran a limo hire company in Edinburgh. Traded a little on the notoriety of his family name, although his father famously had as little to do with his brother as possible, and his sister refused to have the old man's name even mentioned in the family home.

Remembering that David Burns called himself a 'family man'.

Whatever, that notorious uncle probably fascinated young Robert when he was growing up. In our hearts, we're all fascinated by rogues. It's why we keep perpetuating those myths about girls loving bad boys or men secretly desiring to be trouble-makers and lawbreakers.

He climbed in the back of the car and we made eye contact in the rear-view. He pushed his glasses up his nose. I hadn't expected the glasses. Made him look less like a would-be gangster and more a trainee accountant. 'You look as though you've at least read a few books.'

'One or two. They had pictures, though.'

'Can't stand books myself,' he said. 'Novels . . . what the fuck's the point reading about something that never happened?'

I didn't say anything.

'Hey, man, lighten the fuck up!' He rubbed his fingers along the bridge between his upper lip and his nose. As though checking for something there. He was just getting over a bad cold, or he'd just dumped his face into a mountain of flour, still hadn't quite got it all off his face. I figured even money.

He was an unassuming man, round about the belly, and with the kind of face that would start to sag in middle age. He'd probably end up looking a little like David Cameron or the lead from *Midsomer Murders*. In his head, he probably figured himself for Robert De Niro's double. De Niro in his box-office ruling hey-day, naturally.

Something about this assignment felt like a punishment. Maybe Burns had started to cotton on to something approaching the truth, was trying to keep me out the way until he could ascertain the truth of his own suspicions.

What I had done to Findo was a mistake. I knew that. No matter if Findo talked or not, Burns would know he couldn't trust me when push came to shove. Maybe he'd always suspected that. Everyone has lines they won't cross.

I can live with the deaths of those who deserve it.

But there are limits.

Robert gave me an address in the city centre.

85

I set off, doing the whole limo driver bit, not making conversation unless he started it, ensuring I kept my tone disinterested at best. Burns didn't want me to be his nephew's best friend. He just needed to ensure that no one messed with the lad. Robert Burns believed himself to be a hard man. His uncle wasn't so sure.

As I drove, Robert checked his phone in the back seat. Texting. Glasses reflecting the glow of the tiny screen, obscuring his features.

When we arrived, I waited in the car. The address was residential. New build apartments. I offered to check the lay of the land. He laughed it off. 'Anyone who wants my uncle won't come through me. Not here. Who gives a fuck about me here?'

Maybe. Maybe not. But from the little I knew about Robert Burns, he'd made a few efforts to follow in his uncle's footsteps over in Lothian. The limo business was good, but intelligence pointed towards drivers dealing en route and a few less than legal fares being taken without question.

When he came back, he had a girl with him. Couldn't have been more than twenty-five. Dark hair, red dress, good legs. Dressed in the kind of heels that meant she had to lean on Robert for support. The way they walked, I figured they knew each other. Or at least had got intimate over the last few minutes. All power to him working so fast and looking so ordinary.

From the back of the car, Robert introduced the girl to me. Her name was Eileen. She laughed, and I could hear from the birdlike chirp that she was already a little tipsy. 'You don't have a first name?'

'Not that I like to use, no.'

She laughed at that. 'Like Mulder.'

I started the engine.

She said it again. 'Like Mulder. Fox Mulder. *X-Files*. Didn't like his first name, either.'

I said, 'I can understand.'

In the rear-view, Robert had this look I recognized, wondering why the girl was talking to me and not him. Probably best, then, that I stayed quiet.

As I drove, I got more of a feel for this man. Robert Burns liked to think he worked and played hard. He liked girls in red dresses who smelled of cheap perfume. His idea of a night out was meeting old friends at the club that used to be known as the Mardi Gras.

More commonly called, the Manky Bra.

The club had been a real meat market. I'd been in once or twice during my last few years of school, when it was still cool to sneak into the clubs. Then later, when I was working the late beat as a copper. It hadn't seemed much different either way. The unholy trinity of too loud, too crowded, too hot. People getting pissed and aggressive.

The more things change, the more they . . . aye, well, we all know how that one goes. The place hadn't changed too much in the years since I'd last dared go inside. Despite the brand new name and the interior redesign.

On the floor, the music had a physical presence. It thrummed through your bones, set your teeth chattering. So loud, it bent the room. Distorted the world around you.

Made me sick to my stomach.

Before we went in, Robert asked if maybe I could hang back a bit. He didn't want anyone asking questions. He was just some guy out with friends for the night. Kicking back, listening to some tunes, downing a few drinks. Like anyone else. He told me that he didn't want anyone to give a fuck that he was David Burns's nephew. Assured me that no one even knew. Probably.

Part of me was inclined to agree. I'd been given this gig to sideline me for a while. Keep me out of the old man's hair. Such as he had left. Burns wasn't sure he could trust me. He wanted me where I could do the least damage.

Watching his nephew playing at being a gangster for the night was the very definition of busywork.

And the lad really was playing at gangster. Coming out to places like this, dancing with girls in red dresses who were pissed before they even got out their own front door. Swanning into clubs like he owned the place. And every time he went to the bathroom, I knew it wasn't just for a piss. But my job wasn't to monitor his drug intake. I had to make sure that he was safe.

I hung around the edges of the dancefloor. Sipped at never ending water bottles and ignored anyone who tried to talk to me. My eyes always on Robert Burns and his ever-growing crowd.

There were four of them at first, with more gathering round their orbit as the evening went on. They grabbed a bunch of sofas and lounged out.

No one seemed to bother them.

No one bothered me.

Maybe I looked like a bouncer.

Maybe I just looked boring.

'Home, James!'

'Whose home?'

'Mine.'

'Right.'

'You can't come up.'

I was already pulling out. 'Sure.'

'He's got to wait outside?'

'It's my job.'

'Like you have a butler!' That laugh again. Guess good legs and a red dress made up for a lot in the world of Robert Burns.

I kept my eyes on the road. They shut up in the back seat. I considered telling them to put their seatbelts on, but what did I care. I caught flashes of their activity in the rear view, easily resisted the urge to perv. There are some people you just don't want to see getting off, and Robert Burns was one of them. His companion might have been able to pull off attractive when half sober, but sloshed and uncoordinated she just looked plain daft.

Then again, most people lose their dignity in the throes of passion. Throw drink into the mix, and you're laughing.

As she unlocked the door to her place, Robert came back, leaned in against the driver's side window. 'So, like, what are you going to do?'

'I've got plans.'

'Aye?'

'Oh, aye.'

He gave me a wink, trotted off after the girl in the red dress.

I waited until they were inside, switched on the stereo, sat back and let loose a long sigh. Then, I pulled the battered paperback from the glove compartment. *The Killing of the Tinkers.*

Jim White drawled from the speakers. I lost myself in the book, amid the dirt and sleaze of a noir-tinged Galway.

Forgot about my life.

For a little while.

Eighteen

Malone said, 'If I ever suspected anyone would be a turncoat . . . well, it would be you.'

Best I could do was shoot for a poker face. No sense rising to it. He was playing with me. Didn't even care if I was listening.

'Really, if you were a betting man, you'd say, "that cunt McNee, he's the kind of shitebag would rat out his friends."'

'There you go,' I said, finally giving in. 'Shows why you never won the fucking pools.'

'Sure. Right enough.' He didn't know what to do now that I'd responded. Except keep running. He was dressed in jogging bottoms and a white vest, pounding out the miles on the ceaselessly humming treadmill. The sound of the machine and the padding of his feet only amplified the emptiness of the building.

I'd been called out just past six. Escorted inside this faceless, near empty office building, thinking that maybe this was finally the end. Convinced when I saw the expression on Malone's face. It was the kind of expression you were sure would wind up being the last thing you ever saw.

But this wasn't the end. Not for me. Not yet.

'Still can't believe it. You think you know a man . . .'

I knew how he felt. I was still trying to figure it out, put all the pieces together. Clearly Sandy had leaked word that Findo decided to roll over and expose his belly to the cops. Making him public enemy number one in the Burns camp. But what purpose did that serve? Sure, it made me look good in the old man's eyes. But only for a moment. The truth could easily rear its head. Griggs had played a dangerous hand. For me more than him, of course.

What I was beginning to realize: in this game, I was expendable. And there was no end to the board. No way the lowly pawn could become an all-powerful Queen. All I had to look forward to was the endless drudgery of manoeuvring to the front lines until I died.

If, like Ernie before me, I fucked up, Griggs would just find someone else to manipulate.

'Explains a few things,' I said, still trying work out whether what Malone had told me was the truth.

'Like?'

'Why he was nervous with me around. Fin was playing both sides against the middle. He had everyone sussed and then I come in, screw with his head.'

'You're the one screwed in the head.' He spat out the words, working a good sweat. The machine revved faster. Malone got red in the cheeks and across what would once have been his hairline.

'All the same, the boss wants you to keep in with his nephew . . .'

'Babysitting duty?'

'Aye, he doesn't think you're cut out for what he has in mind. Neither do I. Fin may have had the wrong idea about you, but you're still not ready for some of the more . . . hands-on aspects of this little fracas with Nairn.'

'You mean he doesn't think I have what it takes to break some heads?'

'Know your problem, McNee? You still think like polis. Not good guys and bad guys, all that shite. More . . . you've a polis morality. See, you'd put a man in jail – maybe give him a beating, too, but that's alright – when what he really deserves is having barbed wire shoved up his fuckin' piss-hole, know what I'm saying?'

'I'm soft on crime, soft on the causes of crime?'

'Also . . .' He slowed the machine down. The sweat showed through his shirt, now. His dome glistened. His legs quit pumping so hard, taking him down to a walking pace. 'Also, McNee, the fact is that you're a real bloody smartarse. And frankly we'd rather have you not upsetting anyone else. This shite with you and Findo was bad enough, know what I mean?'

I knew what he meant. I wasn't popular. The old man had a soft spot for me, but most folk thought he was mad or senile. Maybe losing his touch. So while the pressure was on, I was to be relegated to the kind of duty where I couldn't do any harm. A pariah in all but name.

Reminded me a little of my time on the force. Towards the end. After the accident in particular. No one had really wanted to work with me. My attitude, apparently. This, despite my reputation as an up-and-comer. But then most people thought my move to CID and the buzz around my name was more to do with my friendship with Ernie Bright than anything else.

No matter what side of the law I was on, I didn't seem to make friends too easily.

But being assigned to look after Rabbie was a real slap in the face.

Like I told Malone, it was babysitting duty. They could dress it up any way they liked, it wouldn't change a bloody thing.

Nineteen

'I'm out.'

'What do you mean, "you're out"?'

'Just temporarily.'

'What do you mean, "you're out"?'

Griggs sat in the car opposite, window down,

engine ticking over. Anyone came by, he was ready to get out and fast. So was I. Face to face meets could be dangerous, but when it came to major developments, they were necessary. There are some things you can't communicate in text or email. Or even down a phone line.

Also, I could see his face. He wasn't taking the news well.

'All this time, this effort, this risk . . .'

'All my risk.'

He looked at me. His eyes betrayed what he was thinking. That kind of anger can't be pushed down. Not for long, anyway.

The man I had known was a good copper. Considered to be one of the best. The good guy with the bad past. Living proof that circumstances don't always predict a man's future.

His father had beaten him. Killed Griggs's mother. The rumour mill said that the young Griggs had killed his father, too. But there was no proof of that, only talk. Station gossip, especially about our own, is rarely worth listening to.

However he started out, Griggs became a good man. And a better policeman. He had a weakness for domestic abuse cases, wading in like he was the hand of God. But then, most cops you talk to have a bug up their arse when it comes to certain kinds of criminal act. He was known for his even-handedness, for his honesty, for his ability to work – more or less – within the confines allowed by the law. He made enemies along the way of course – a crooked politician once tried to set him up on a corruption charge – but when you're police, you can't help making enemies. And when you have the kind of zeal that Griggs had, sometimes those enemies are going to try and take you out any way they can.

The man in the other car no longer had the eyes of a good man. He looked at me like he wanted to crush me beneath his shoe and walk on. I was worthless. Useless. Meant nothing to him. He was fuelled by anger. Bitterness. Didn't care about anything except achieving the singular goal of getting revenge on David Burns. He wanted the bad man to suffer. And he didn't care about the cost of achieving that.

So what was I doing allowing this man to manipulate me? Why had I let him bully me into betraying principles I would have fought for in years gone by?

Because of his reputation? Because of the man he used to be?

Griggs wasn't that man any more. And I was beginning to realize that. Maybe he never had been. Maybe everyone had deluded themselves about the kind of man he really was. Or maybe he just changed. Slowly. Incrementally. In ways that no one would really notice.

Susan had told me that Griggs and I were alike in many ways. Maybe once. Certainly, I once had that same sense of focus, that same hatred of the universe and everyone in it. That same intensity.

How had people looked at me?

Had they seen the same look in my eyes that I saw in his?

'Do you think there's a chance that you'll get back in?' he asked.

'With Burns? I don't know. Your little stunt with Findo has them watching their back. Jesus, what the fuck did you do?'

'You'd rather he told them what he told us? That you were a traitor? That you took the side of the men you had been sent to hurt?'

'He wanted to kill them. What was I supposed to do?'

'Whatever it took not to fuck up your cover.'

'You were in my shoes, you would cross the line?'

There was a moment of silence. In the distance, there was the slow rushing sound of traffic crossing the bridge. Car headlights illuminated us for a moment on their way past. But no one came into the car park. No one joined us. This time of night, the only people looking for other vehicles in deserted places like this were doggers and undercover police.

'Don't talk to me about lines, McNee. Don't tell me you won't kill. Don't tell me you haven't killed.'

Using my own past against me. The way he had from the first time he barged into my office.

'You know what's at stake here,' he said. 'You know why we're doing this.'

'I know why I'm doing this. But this isn't like you, Griggs.'

'Yeah?'

'We worked together. I remember who you were.'

'One time only. You were in uniform back them. The rules were different.'

'And so were you.'

'I was more innocent.'

'You were a DI.'

'So?'

What was the point in arguing? He was in control. Same as he had always been. Except back then I had trusted men like Griggs with my life.

And now?

I didn't trust anyone.

Especially men like Griggs.

Men who lied and manipulated. Believed they were on the side of the angels. Called themselves the good guys. Believed the label entitled them to do whatever it took to achieve that end.

Griggs took my silence for capitulation. 'There's going to be a war,' he said. 'And it's your fault if it escalates.'

'What do you want from me? I've given you everything.'

'I need cast iron—'

'—No,' I said. 'Between what I have and the evidence I know Ernie gathered, you've got more than enough to take the old man out. There's something else going on. And you need to tell me.'

He looked about to say something. His lips curled. His incisors showed. But he bit back whatever response he had.

I let it go.

What else could I do?

He said, 'Get close to Burns. Place him at the murder of Jason Taylor. Place him at as many killings as you can. The ones he did personally, the ones he ordered. Not just your word. Definitive proof. I want him on tape. I want him to confess to murder. No more hearsay, no more we-said-he-said. Nothing a lawyer can twist to the point of reasonable doubt. No more Not-Proven verdicts. I want the truth. From his mouth to God's bastard ears.'

'With you playing the part of Our Lord?'

Griggs shook his head, peeled out of the parking space and took the turn on to the road back to the bridge far too fast.

I watched his car vanish into the black.

Realized I was alone.

Twenty

'McNee, ya crazy bollocks!' Robert reached over from the back seat to clap me on the shoulder. His long fingers wrapped round me. I thought of the film, *Nosferatu*. Tried not to shiver too hard. 'Good to see you again.'

'You too,' I said, not bothering to sound like I meant it. Like he would give a toss. 'Where's the girl tonight?'

'New night,' he said.

'New girl?'

'You were young once, right?'

'Still am.'

'So maybe this one's got a friend.'

'Thought we had established boundaries,' I said.

'Aye, you're not my friend.'

'I'm not even here. I'm the invisible man.'

He settled back. Even in the rear view I could see that he'd been drinking. His eyes were glazed over. The night was young. A few hours, and he'd be wide-eyed and tripped out.

I drove us to the city centre, parked down on Brown Street near the old student halls of residence. Remembered being called out to them every so often as a uniform to investigate petty theft and the occasional recreational drugs charge.

I kept my pace slow, remaining a few feet behind Robert as he swaggered up towards the club. Jesus, he claimed to have come to the city to see his uncle, and all he did was go out and get high. Maybe half an eye on making the old man's connections. After all, Burns wasn't getting any younger and when he did eventually cark it there was going to be a power vacuum in the North East. Maybe wee Rabbie wasn't as spaced out as I first suspected. Maybe he was smarter than he looked. Wouldn't be too hard.

He met some folk in the queue. The way they acted, they knew each other well. I didn't recognize them, but figured they were his crew over round these parts. Guys who liked hanging around with someone they thought was a bit dangerous. I kept my distance, but made sure I got in a word with the guys on the door. One of them knew me. We'd met at SIA conferences over the years. Got on well enough and we'd had some drinks at the bar, but our professional relationship existed only within the confines of anodyne hotel bars and overheated conference rooms.

'Heard your licence got suspended.'

'ABI,' I said. 'And it's a temporary thing. I can still work as an investigator.'

'Right.'

'Come on, Brownlie. You know me.'

He gave a tip of the head that was noncommittal at best. His arms were folded. Showing off the black and white tats on his biceps. Even in the depths of winter, he wore short sleeves just so he could show off the ink.

'I know you, alright' he said. 'You moody wee fuck.'

He had me on that score. We'd met during the dark days, when all I'd been interested in was burying myself in work, forgetting who I was. I hadn't been looking to make friends, and I guess it had been more than obvious. You hadn't needed to be Sherlock Holmes to work that one out.

'Right-oh,' he said. 'They get in, you get in. I know how it is. Besides, what they're saying about you, I figure I still have to go with my gut. Which says you're all right.'

'Even if I am a moody wee fuck?'

He shrugged. 'But if they start something and you don't shut it down . . .'

'Sure, sure.'

'Want a smoke?'

I laughed, shook my head.

'You aren't all bad, then? Fuck, you gone vegetarian, too?'

'Not to say I wouldn't kill for one some days.'

'You're only human.'

'Right.'

Brownlie let us through without incident.

As before, I spent most of the night walking

the floor, wishing I was anywhere else. Preferably somewhere with soundproofing.

Or a torture chamber. That might have been better. Relentless white noise blasted through headphones would have beaten the relentless boom-boom-boom that echoed through the crowd of dancers, vibrating their bodies and minds. The ones that had both.

About an hour or so into the evening, someone stood next to me. Arms folded. About as relaxed as a cat in a box full of angry dogs. Not looking at me, but making sure I knew she was there. The kind of pose only another copper would recognize.

'DI Kellen,' I shouted, bending down to yell into her ear over the thump-thump. 'Nice to see you know how to enjoy yourself.'

'Go to hell,' she shouted back. Not looking at me. Watching the floor. Eyes on Robert and his friends. The grim determination you might associate with a bird of prey. There had always been something of the hawk in her features: a sharpness that made her seem alert and utterly focussed.

Her colleagues called her single minded. They meant it as a compliment.

'So what are you drinking?' I asked. Sarcasm high on the agenda.

'Water. Otherwise I might be tempted to jump your bones.'

'Not sure I'd resist.'

'Except you're a gentleman.'

'Sure. There's that.'

She shifted weight from foot to foot,

deliberately out of time with the beat of the bass. 'So why don't we quit the flirting?'

'Why not? The night's not going to end with you cuffing me to the bedpost.'

'It wouldn't be the bedpost.' Hard to tell in amid the flashing strobes whether she was smiling. 'So, what, this is legitimate work for you?'

'I'm a tax payer.'

'Who's been suspended from a professional body, accused of unlawful conduct.'

'You don't have a case to make.'

'They took the case away from me.'

'You sound paranoid.'

'I am. Somebody up there likes you.'

'And you don't like that?'

'Anyone assisted by divine intervention is suspicious, McNee.'

'So you're not a believer, then?' She didn't say anything. 'I wouldn't call it divine intervention, DI Kellen. More that someone saw sense.' On the dance floor, Robert was throwing shapes. Dangerously big shapes to throw in a space where people were pressed so close together. 'You never told me who set you on to me in the first place.'

'I like lost causes,' she said. 'Catch the ones who got away.' She thought about that for a second. 'The ones who think they got away.'

'And that's me, is it?'

'One among many.'

'Nice to feel special.'

The whole time I had one eye on Robert. A moment's distraction could result in serious trouble. First thing you learned about close protection was that your eye always had to be on the target. No matter what else was happening. And sure enough, some guy was giving Robert the look. The one that says, 'stop being a dick.' Robert was oblivious. His friends were whooping and hollering.

'Never a quiet moment,' Kellen said.

'We'll see.' It wasn't a situation yet. Just one guy shaking his head. Hardly a riot.

'My problem with you,' she said, 'is not rumour. It's the people you hang around with. Like you want us to look at you a certain way. Showing off your guilt. Flaunting it.'

On the dance floor, the man with the pissed-off face had finally got Robert's attention. They were squaring up. The kind of swaggering confrontation most guys have after a few pints. Already a space had formed around them on the floor.

I tried not to sigh. At least, not obviously.

Didn't stop Kellen laughing as I stepped forward.

She yelled something at me over the music. But I didn't hear it. Didn't need to. Whatever it was, it wasn't exactly a compliment.

I ran down on to the floor. Robert was on his tiptoes. He and Mr Angry were forehead to chin, testosterone leaking like a nuclear reactor in meltdown. People were giving them a wide berth. A few lads on the edge were shouting encouragement. They wanted to see blood.

The main rule of any close protection gig is this: get between your target and any potential threat. Even if your target is the one causing the aggro in the first place.

The guy was big. I'd seen that from the other

side of the room. But up close, he was a truly solid bastard. The kind of chest that came from pumping weights. The kind of arms that would make Schwarzenegger jealous. Not that it mattered. When it comes to a fight, it's not always the big man who wins. Witness enough punters kicking off on a Saturday night, and you learn that lesson fast. Size is intimidating, but it's not an indication of superiority.

The big guy said, 'Who the fuck're you?'

'The one telling you to back off.'

'You a bouncer?'

I didn't say anything.

'Your friend was being a cunt.'

Again, I kept quiet. Stood my ground.

'Aye, well, so . . . right . . . tell him he dances like a queer.' The big man backed down. Hesitantly. I could sense disappointment from the spectators hoping for a rammie. It was a physical thing. an oppressive and disappointing sensation. Maybe enough to encourage one or the other of us to give it a go. But drunk as the big man was, he knew he'd been beaten. More, he knew that I wasn't playing hard man. He was pissed, but not enough to get into a fight he couldn't win.

Sometimes all it takes to win a fight is attitude.

'Aye, run away, yah prick!'

And sometimes all it takes to pick a fight is an attitude.

Robert had barely finished yelling at the big man before he moved. Luckily drink made the big man sluggish. Like facing down a tank: he had size on his side, but no speed and no grace.

I sidestepped him, brought my fist down low and into his balls. He doubled, stumbled, and collapsed.

A dirty move? Maybe, but it ended the situation fast. Brownlie could clear up the mess. I just wanted to get the fuck out of there as fast as I could.

I took advantage of the situation. Hustled Robert off the floor fast as I could. He was shouting over his shoulder the whole time. I got him out the fire exit, slammed him against a wall and pressed my hand over his face. 'Shut the fuck up!'

I let go. We were out in an alley at the rear of the club. The night air was sharp. The kind of sharp that could slice open a vein. It got to Robert fast. He struggled to catch his breath, then doubled up and vomited. His sick was the kind of bright orange that you only get late at night. Spattered my shoes and the bottom of my jeans.

'Jesus!'

'Oh fuck me, I'm sorry, man. So fuckin' sorry. I mean, fuck . . .'

He shuddered and then collapsed to his knees. Started to sob. Like a wee boy who's suddenly realized the very real trouble that he's in. There was an apologetic tone to his tears, a forced realization of his own idiocy.

The sad cry of the drunk.

And I fell for it. I'd been young and stupid once. And for all his swagger, all his trading off his uncle's name, he was little more than a guy trying to have a good time, not really aware of the consequences of his own actions.

His friends, I noted, were nowhere to be seen.

'Come on,' I said, offering my hand down to him. 'We'll go back to yours, get some coffee on, forget about it. Aye?'

He took the hand offered. Let me haul him to his feet.

Twenty-One

Robert held on to me as we walked. Barely able to manage a straight line. Not pissed, but also embarrassed. His breath came in short bursts. A panic attack, perhaps. A sudden realization of what he had done. An epiphany of sorts. Wouldn't last long. Give him a night of sleep, he'd dismiss the incident as a momentary lapse: a drink-fuelled anxiety that he didn't need to worry about.

But these things always run deeper. I knew that better than most.

'I always looked up to him,' he said. 'My uncle. Wasn't supposed to, like, but who doesn't love a gangster?'

'He's a businessman,' I said. But even I couldn't lie to a drunk man.

'Piss off. You work for him. You know the truth. You . . . know . . . like . . .' Beginning to mumble, trailing off at the end of sentences, thoughts fading before they completed themselves.

I didn't say anything. Just ensured that he stayed upright as we limped past the police station and down to the traffic lights. Just a short hop across the road and we'd be back at the car. Then I could take him home, tuck him up and get some rest.

But I knew I'd be sleeping on his couch. Couldn't leave him alone in this state. No matter how much of a prick he was or who his uncle happened to be, he was still a client. Which made him my responsibility. Something I took seriously.

It would be easy to dismiss Robert Burns as not worth the effort. But repulsive as he was to me, he was still a human being. With all the flaws that implied. He was trying to live up to an ideal he could never match. He would never be like his uncle, and he knew it. He'd always be a wee boy playing at being a gangster, never with the balls to be the real thing. Men like his uncle were not made or created. They were born that way. They couldn't help who they were. Just as a man like Robert Burns couldn't help being a wannabe. He would always be running to play catch up with the big boys. His reality could never match his ambition. And in a way, I felt sorry for him because of that.

The minute you stop trying to look for the humanity in people, you've already lost. I had known monsters in my time, people whose actions and perversions had made them into outcasts from the world. And yet every time, I had seen in them a glimpse of who they might have been, who they could have been, if they had not given in to the worst of themselves.

Robert Burns was no monster. Just a guy with

an inferiority complex and an uncle he admired. For all the wrong reasons.

We crossed the Marketgait, waiting for the green man, not risking Robert's slow progress on the roads that rushed up between the station and the old Tay Mills. We were in the very centre of the city and yet at this time of night, cars treated the road like a racetrack, bombing up and down with little thought for pedestrians or other road users.

The irony of the police station's presence was all too obvious.

We walked down the roughly cobbled street at the side of the Mills, round to the car park at the rear of the building. A woman walked past us, smiling at me as she did so. Early forties or late thirties, tall, with bobbed blonde hair and an understated dress sense. She didn't look like she'd been out on the piss. Maybe she was getting geared up. Or heading home after a late night at the office.

'Your pal looks a little worse for wear.'

'You know how it is.'

She nodded. 'You driving, then?'

'Designated.'

'Poor bugger.' Smiling a little too much. Maybe she had been drinking, was just one of those people who hid it well. Some people, they get drunk, they only hint at it when they smile. 'You, I mean.'

'I'll have a belt when I get home.'

'Bet you will. You boys have a blast.' She toddled past, throwing a wee wink. Flirtatious? Perhaps. It was that time of night. But still, I figured it was bold for a woman to stop and chat

108

to two drunk strangers in a side street that was half-lit at best. Maybe the presence of the police station just a few feet away made her feel safe. Or maybe she just didn't give a toss. Maybe we didn't look that dangerous.

I pulled Robert to the car. He leaned on the hood while I unlocked the door. Gulping in the night air.

Something about the woman was bothering me. I couldn't stop thinking about her. And not in that way. Paranoid, maybe. Tired. Jumping at shadows. The work getting to me. When you're waiting to be found out twenty-four hours a day, seven days a week, you can be forgiven moments of unjustified uncertainty.

'McNee!'

I turned. Kellen. Following us. Feet clicking on the cobbles where we'd just walked.

'I just want to have a wee chat.'

'This isn't a good time.' I stepped away from the car. Leaving the key in the driver's side lock. Robert was still leaning on the hood, drawing breaths, trying to convince himself that he really was alright.

I didn't want him to hear any conversation I might have with Kellen, no matter how pissed he was. How likely to forget.

I met her halfway. Far enough from the car that Robert wouldn't be able to earwig with ease. 'What the hell do you want?'

'We never finished our conversation.'

'This isn't a good time.'

'Just wanted to let you know, you're not getting off lightly.'

Hammering the point home with a mallet. I graciously decided not to point that out to her. 'He's a client. Long as he doesn't break the law in my presence, I have an obligation to—'

'Don't give me that, McNee. Just . . . just don't.' She shook her head. 'I'm beginning to think you actually believe your own bullshit.'

There had been moments over the last seven or eight months I'd just wanted to yell at someone, tell them the whole damn story. But I couldn't. I was undercover. All the way. Walking a line where I couldn't see how far the drop was on either side.

Kellen had been riding me even before I agreed to work for Griggs. She saw only what she'd been told to see. Focussed only on what backed up her truth.

If I was going to yell at anyone, I wanted to yell at her. Loud enough that there'd be no question of her not understanding. I wanted her to see the truth. Needed her to see it. She was a good cop. Her sense of morality was on the money. I needed her not to think of me as one of the bad guys. To know that I was doing the wrong things for the right reasons.

But to tell her would be suicide. Professional. Personal. Maybe literal.

'You don't get it do you?' I said. 'That sometimes you don't see everything. You don't—'

I heard the noise of a car door slamming. Turned round to see Robert in the driver's seat.

'Fucksakes!' I took a step forward.

The engine coughed. Of course it did. I'd left the fucking keys in the driver's door.

Again.

The cough. The catch.

He was going to drive home drunk. Last thing I needed was for a man connected to David Burns to be found in my car and incapable of driving.

I made to run. Hands out, signalling him to just fucking well stop.

Didn't even manage the first step.

It was the second time in my life I'd been caught in the path of a bomb. The second time I'd been unprepared.

But I knew what was happening. Realized as the world slowed down. The punch in the centre of my chest, the feeling of rising heat, the sensation of weightlessness. Déjà vu all over again.

I slammed back into Kellen. We tumbled. Landed hard on the dashed pebble surface of the car park.

I closed my eyes.

Exhaled.

Inhaled.

Tasted ashes in the air.

Twenty-Two

Ewan 'Sooty' Soutar was beside the bed when I opened my eyes. I'd been drifting in and out since the doctors checked me over. My chest was tight, skin stretched across bone. A reaction to what had happened. I was in shock. So they said.

111

'Jesus fuck, Steed,' Sooty said. 'Every time we talk, you're in the shite.'

No kidding.

Sooty looked the same as ever: dangerous. Big. More muscle than fat, although you might be forgiven for thinking otherwise in the wrong light. He shaved his head, had a goatee that gave his face a hard edge. Looked like a bouncer more than a cop. Used to moonlight as one, in fact. But since he got promoted to DI, he'd devoted his whole life to the force. Seemed happier for it, too. Happy as Sooty could seem, anyway. He wasn't much of one for smiling. Not around me, anyway,

'Guess I'm just unlucky,' I said. Each word ripped the back of my throat. I wanted to cough up the lining.

'Aye, right.' He took a deep breath, pulled out his notebook. 'So let's have it, then. What happened?'

'Kellen?'

'She's fine. Just had a wee chat with her.'

'And?'

'And now I'm having a wee chat with you. You know how this works, Steed. So answer the questions. Then we can catch up. But if you're interested, she didn't ask how you were doing.'

Sure.

'The question?' I said. My memory was fritzed. There was a ringing in my ears. Somewhere just beneath that, I could hear the echo what might have been a scream. Sounded a lot like Rabbie Burns on fire.

'Just tell me what happened tonight.'

'The car blew up.'

'Aye, we get that. You know that this is the second time you've been found in the presence of an incendiary device attached to a motor vehicle? Once is unlucky . . .'

'Last time it was Molly came to see me.' Meaning DI Molly Mollinson. Hard man, despite the name. Suffered from 'Boy-Named-Sue' syndrome, but still a good copper. 'He's given up on me, then? Or was it just that you drew the short straw this time?'

'You always had an attitude. Lately it's been worse, though. Something you want to talk about?'

'Not really. We were never that close, Sooty. Even before you tried to rip my head off.' Sooty's temper could get the better of him. When he thought I was responsible for landing a senior officer in a coma, he hadn't even asked me to explain myself.

'Then let's talk about the bomb.'

'Someone placed it while we were in the club.'

'Meaning they knew you were there?'

'Guess so.'

'Meaning they knew Robert was there?'

'He's the likeliest target.'

'I don't know, Steed. I can think of more than a few people who'd like to blow your arse into a million pieces.'

'Most of them cops.'

'Aye, that's the problem.' He shook his head. 'But, for the sake of expediency and all that shite, I'm going to assume this wasn't a copper.'

'I wouldn't assume anything. Wouldn't even let you off the hook right now.'

113

He looked ready to say something but held back. Maybe remembering how the last few times we'd talked, I'd been the man he blamed for fucking over other officers.

Safe to say that me and Sooty were never going to be friends.

'You need to tell me anything. Did you see anyone hanging around the car before the incident?' He was keeping it calm. Professional. What's it that they say about flies and honey?

'Other than Kellen?'

Again that catch in his expression. 'Other than Kellen.'

I thought about it. Back before the explosion. It was tough. My memory was caught in a groove, like an old vinyl with a deep scratch and the needle stuck in place.

I jerked the needle.

The track jumped back too far.

In the club. Getting between Robert and the big guy. The hint of fear as everything was about to kick off.

Jesus, the fucker could have broken my neck with his pinkie. Who would have thought false bravado and sobriety would win the day?

I jerked the needle again. Caught another groove. Closer this time. Before the explosion. Before Kellen.

The woman I'd thought was a little drunk. That smile playing around her lips. Flirtatious. But gently mocking.

You boys have a blast.

Don't tell me there's no such thing as a coincidence.

'Anyone?'

I shook my head. 'No one.' My voice sounded thick, and I was in danger of biting my own tongue when I closed my mouth. Like the first signs of drunkenness creeping in. But I hadn't touched a drop all evening.

The drugs kicking in. Finally. My body too light. My eyes too heavy.

I said. 'I didn't see anything out of the ordinary.' Struggling to remember the words.

Sooty didn't believe me. I had this idea that I was a good liar, but anyone would be off their game when they'd just been blown off their feet by a car bomb.

Still, he didn't push it. Maybe wary after our last few encounters. Not sure if he'd want to murder me when I told the truth.

'Play it your way,' he said. 'Watch the wall while the gentlemen go by. Pretend you know nothing. But don't expect any favours from me.'

'I never would.'

'You're playing a dangerous game. You know that much. Right?'

'Aye. The game's always dangerous.'

He shook his head, closed the notepad and stood up. 'We'll talk again.'

'I look forward to it.'

'Oh.' He raised his eyebrows. 'I doubt that, Steed. I really do.'

Twenty-Three

I was discharged the next morning with mild bruising and no more than a few scrapes down my back. They burned when I pulled on a shirt. I didn't mind. I was getting used to the pain. We were old friends, now.

I took the bus to the city centre, gingerly spreading my weight across the seat, aware of every ache and tingle. The drugs don't work? Aye, imagine how I'd be feeling without them.

Back at the flat, I checked the second mobile, the one hidden behind the couch with the laptop. Six messages from Susan. I answered with one: 'I'm OK.'

Griggs had sent only one message.

'Call me.'

Aye, the very measure of concern.

I didn't call him. Instead, I ran the shower hot as I could and stood in the steam until I couldn't stand it any longer. I'm a sucker for a strong shower. The pounding of the water. The white noise that becomes a haven. For a few minutes, I can be cut off from the world. I can exist as myself. Alone.

I came out and towelled down gingerly. My body ached. My muscles strained. The cuts and grazes in my back were raw, pulsating. Reminded me of their presence with the insistence of an ignored toddler.

I got dressed in a fresh shirt and jeans. Was half done buttoning up when the buzzer went. I answered, already knowing whose finger was on the button.

Malone didn't waste time on false concern. Just took one look at me and said, 'You get a simple task and it winds up being a bloodbath. This is getting to be a habit with you.'

'How's the old man taking it?'

'Why don't you come and find out for yourself?'

Now there was an offer you couldn't refuse.

'Animals!'

The old man raging. Face scarlet. Veins pulsing in the right side of his head. Ready to throttle someone. Anyone. He had always suppressed this kind of anger in my presence. But I'd known it was there.

I understood how he had got his reputation. I could see the thug – maybe even the killer – he had once been.

It reached to the primal part of my brain, made me want to run.

But I didn't.

'Animals!' He paced. Kicked up dust from the floor of the disused office space. Stomped over to an old pine desk and gripped it underneath. 'Animals!' He threw the desk over. Making the kind of sound you could have heard over the noise of a Spinal Tap gig.

These days, he looked his age, but there was still something of the old strength inside David Burns. He had been fuelled by anger in his youth.

117

Still had it in him, despite his claims to the contrary.

Malone and I stood in silence by the door. Let him scream and rage. Talk to himself. Rant. Roar. When he finally acknowledged our presence, he spoke to me directly. Maybe because he had already told Malone what he had to say or maybe because he trusted me. As he always said, we had a kinship.

'He was nobody. He was innocent.'

Hardly. But in the things that mattered, Robert Burns had really been a nobody. Taking him out like that was senseless. Served no purpose. But then, maybe that was the point.

'There are rules.'

Rules that even Burns had broken over and over again. But I didn't tell him that. He believed completely in the rules when they suited him. Like a religious zealot who covets his neighbour's wife, worships false idols and still does not see his own hypocrisy.

'Unwritten?'

He laughed. 'They don't need to be written. It's what separates us from the psychopaths. You don't hurt a man's family. Not unless they're involved. Not unless they're soldiers.'

'Then we're at war?' Using 'we' without even thinking. I was beginning to empathize with the old man. See things from his point of view. Losing my sense of perspective.

'Always.'

He turned away. Hunched over and shivered. Crying? I couldn't be sure. When he turned back to face me, his eyes were red. But from anger or sadness I couldn't really say.

Family is a funny thing. We can hate them. We can despise them, and yet still love them.

They had killed his nephew. Without warning. Crossed the line.

God only knew what the old man would do, now.

'They've forgotten,' Burns said. 'Forgotten who I am. They see a frail old fucker. They've forgotten the lessons their fathers fucking learned.'

'No,' I said. 'They know who you are. That's why—'

'You don't understand, McNee. Don't know you ever will. In your way, you're like them. Only aware of an old man with a reputation.'

A reputation for cruelty and hatred. A man who once nailed a priest to a cross over an unpaid debt. Whose idea of mercy had been leaving behind a hammer to pry loose the nails.

'Then tell me.'

'When I was young, my guts burned with ambition. There was nothing I wouldn't do to get what I wanted. I lost some of that when I got older. That's what success does. Dulls fire. Dulls the edge of your soul. Makes you forget the very things you were fighting for in the first place.'

'And now?'

'Now I'm an old man. Cautious. To these lads, I'm little more than a stepping stone. One more corpse they have to step over to get wherever it is they're going.'

'They are what you were.'

'No,' he said. 'They think they're worse.'

'And are they?'

'Son, these little shitebags don't know what

kind of hell they're about to face. They killed my brother's boy. They broke the rules. They'll learn . . . there's always a price.'

The old man could be decent, in his own way, to those he felt deserved it. Callous when it came to those he didn't care about one way or another. But when you crossed him, his wrath was righteous, terrifying and indiscriminate.

His anger had not faded with youth. It had merely retreated. Gone into hibernation. But the death of his nephew had reawakened the old terror. A monster was roaring, raising its head.

It was a warning. A dark sign of things to come.

Twenty-Four

Craig Nairn.

Small time hood. No one important. A charge sheet like so many others. Petty shite, mostly. Some jail time. Suspended sentence. Bad hair. Worse skin. A line in shellsuits and white trainers with knock-off branding on the side. Liked to call people 'Slick'. Saw it in a Hollywood movie and thought it was bad-ass. One of the reasons he got picked up on three muggings, calling people 'Slick', people remembering the way it sounded, his nasal tones mangling the inherent cool he'd been aiming for. He was the kind of prick who blamed bad luck every time he got pinched, failed to see that he was simply incompetent.

He thought he was Tom Sizemore in *Heat*, but looked more like Joe Pesci. Gone to seed.

So what was Nairn doing running an underground people smuggling operation? Busting in on Burns's territories? Arranging a car bomb just to send a message? None of this was consistent with his history.

He wasn't working alone.

He couldn't be.

Didn't have the *nous*.

So who? Who was his backer? His silent partner?

I couldn't stop thinking about the woman. The way she'd smiled at me.

Something about her made alarm bells ring in my brain. She was the one who planted the bomb. Had to be. But female explosive experts were rare. At least, statistically speaking. If it was her, then I figured someone had to know who she was.

To find her, I'd be fishing in a shallow pool. Odds were, if she was contracted, then someone somewhere knew her name and her reputation. To send a message like that, you don't subcontract to an unknown quantity. Not when you run an operation like the one muscling in on the old man's turf.

So I went fishing. Called in old favours.

Went to Perth prison for a meeting with a firebug I arrested years ago. Twitchy little bollocks by the name of Teale. Had a rat-like face and a habit of biting his nails down so short they kept bleeding. He'd suck at the blood, too. Like that was going to stop it coming. Or maybe he liked to think he had vampiric tendencies.

He sat across from me, wagging his head back and forth, maybe thinking that made him look confident. Like most criminals, his self-image was at odds with the way he actually looked.

'You retired, then?' he said. 'Or they threw you out?'

I could smell his breath across the other side of the table. As though his tongue was rotting inside his mouth.

He'd been inside over eight years. Missed my meltdown. But word would have reached him. The gossip in prison walls stretches with desperation for news of the outside world. 'You know the story already,' I said.

'Aye, and it's a doozy.' Nibbled at his left ring finger. 'Killer.'

Word travels. Even when that word is unproven.

I said, 'Sure. I killed a man. In self-defence. You killed families.'

'They were accidental deaths.' Another delicate little chew. Then he looked up and smiled. 'Some of them.'

'You set fire to their houses.'

He shrugged.

Most of Teale's career had been murder for hire. But he was a true-blue pyromaniac. Liked to watch things burn. Got lucky that his personal perversion could turn a profit. Teale reticent about his client list when they finally got him. With a few notable exceptions. After all, there is rarely honour among thieves, however hard they might try to convince you otherwise.

There's even less of it among arsonists.

'I want to talk to you about others of your kind.'

'Of my kind?'

'Arsonists.'

He licked his lips. 'Pyromaniacs.'

'Pyromania is a rare condition.'

'That's why we're like family. No one else can really understand.'

'You said that when you killed people, it was an accident.'

'The families, yes.'

'The families of those you targeted.'

'You know . . . it didn't really matter to me. They were just . . . they were unlucky, I suppose.'

'It was about the fire.'

'It always is. For us.'

He used to hang around internet chat rooms. The ones on the dark side of the net. The ones where you only got in by knowing the right people, the right words, the right attitude. The dark net is real. Look hard enough online, you'll find communities for almost every perversion you can think of. Most of them hidden. Most of them anonymous.

'I'm looking for a woman.'

'Thought you were looking for a fellow pyro.'

'I know the statistics. Ninety percent of arsonists are male.'

'And young.'

'You're not young anymore.'

He thought about that. 'No, I'm not. It's horrible, to look in the mirror, see that grey slipping in around the temples. I thought maybe I'd look sophisticated. Cary Grant, you know? *North by Northwest*.' He flashed yellow choppers. I tried not to breath in, catch another whiff of his breath.

123

'No such luck,' I said.

'Still, I have a certain something.'

And that's why I'd made sure there was a table between us. In case that something was catching.

'I had the guard pull your phone records.'

'I call my mother every Sunday.'

'Your mother's dead.'

'Wondered why she didn't answer.'

'You made four calls to one number in particular. A mobile. It's dead, now. Like your mother. Of course. We think you were talking to someone called Craig Nairn.'

'There's a nice Scottish name. Not exactly feminine though.' He tipped his head to one side. Making me play this one out. My time was precious. His stretched out in front of him. For men like Teale, life could really mean life. No one wanted him on the outside. Not even the social workers who had regular meetings with him. He was the kind of psychopath who couldn't hide. His banal evil was a second skin. Slimy. A corpse dredged from the bogs. He knew it, too. Delighted in the way he made people feel.

When we pulled him in all those years ago, he'd smiled all the way to the station, sitting in the back of the Jam Sandwich, stretching his lips over his teeth in what might have been a smile.

'The two of you shared a youth officer back in the eighties. You and Nairn. You knew each other.'

'That's a leap, Mr McNee.' Emphasizing the 'Mr', letting me know that he was no longer afraid of me now that I no longer held rank. Not

124

that he ever had been, of course. 'Two lads who shared a probation officer decide to become best friends and later on in life they arrange to torch the fuck out of some would-be tough guy from Edinburgh. Sounds like one of those touching wee films you see late at night. Channel 4, maybe. BBC 2.'

'Aye, it does,' I said. 'And you're right. That wee tale would be a stretch. If we didn't have previous record of correspondence between you and Nairn.'

'What did we talk about, then?'

'He wanted a job done.'

'Aye,' he said. Held out his hands. Palms up. Wrists exposed. 'It's a fair cop. I talked to the lad. He asked me if I could arrange something. I told him, no. How could I? I was inside.'

'So you gave him a name. A contact. A fellow pyro. A member of the family.'

'Nah. Besides, how the fuck would I know anyone these days? They monitor what you do online, you know. If you're allowed on at all.' He let his arms flop. Then pulled the right one up to nibble at the nail of his index finger.

'The name of someone who wouldn't be known to the police. The name of someone that could remain anonymous.'

'What you're digging for, is it this lassie you think is a fellow pyro?'

I knew a guy on the *Dundee Herald*. Cameron Connelly. A reporter. From time to time he did me favours. We might be friends if our relationship wasn't purely utilitarian. He once told me that when you go in to interview a subject, it

125

works best if you don't ask questions to which you don't already know the answers.

In other words:

Do your research.

I knew who I was looking for. Looking for a female pyro means fishing in a shallow pool. Most investigative work is trawling through information, sifting for the nuggets you can use. After a while you get good at finding what you don't even know that you're looking for.

Like a name in a file of known associates.

A name no one else would look twice at.

'Four years ago, you corresponded with a woman by the name of Gemma Fairstead. She was one of those prison groupies. Contacted you online through a group known as Prison Chicks.'

'Oh,' Teale said. 'Her.'

'You two hit it off.'

'You've seen the records, then? Of our wee chats?'

I didn't say anything.

'Gives *Fifty Shades* a wee run for its money, aye? Maybe I should publish some of those letters. Might give a few of those sex-starved wifies a thrill to read what me and her were talking about doing to each other.'

'She shared your fascination.' Their messages weren't just about sex. There was fireplay, too. Talk of burning flesh, cauterising wounds. The same tone others might have used to talk about bondage and S&M. But theirs was an even more peculiar kink.

Fire and sex.

What they had in common.

'You never met,' I said. 'Never in the flesh.'

'Oh, but if we had . . .'

'Some of these women, they marry prisoners.'

'Conjugal rights.'

'Well?'

'Well, we figured why spoil what we have?'

'Also you lied about how you looked.'

'It's the internet. We can be anyone we want. That's the modern world, McNee. Nothing's what it seems. Appearance doesn't matter anymore. Not in the digital.'

'Wonder whether she'd have been excited smelling the grease from your burning flesh as she was thinking about burning the toned skin of George Clooney.'

'I said we have the same eyes. That's all.'

And the rest.

'So the relationship went the way they all do?'

'Of course.'

'But she was a firebug like you. Had a thing for explosive blazes. The big bang, right?'

'You did read our letters. Naughty boy.'

'She killed a man last night.'

'How do you know?'

'I saw her.'

'Tell the cops.'

'This isn't about the cops.'

'It's not?'

I leaned forward. Voice low. 'You said it yourself. I'm no longer police. And if you've been keeping your ear to the ground like I think you have, you'll know who I work for.'

'Wondered when you'd get to throwing the old man's name around.'

'I'm a messenger. He knows what I know.'

'Nah. Nah.' But he was shaking. No longer biting his nails. Picking at them. Not sucking the blood, just letting it swell at the grooves around his fingertips. He understood what I was telling him. And he would never say anything, but it scared the shite out of him.

'You said it yourself. Earlier. I killed a man. Shot him.'

'That was . . . I mean it was about . . . Your wife . . .'

'Fiancée, but it doesn't matter. Something like that happens, it changes you.'

'Not like . . .'

'What did you hear about me?'

'That you killed a man. Shot him in the chest.'

'Why did I shoot him?'

'There were stories.'

'Do you believe them?'

He bit his upper lip. Turned his head so he didn't have to look at me. I leaned forward, made sure I was in his eyeline. 'Do you believe them?'

'You were police. You were . . .'

'Look me in the eyes, tell me whether you think I killed a man? Tell me if you think I would do it again.'

He looked at me.

I spent years denying my darker side. Fooled myself with morality and ethical justification. Acted like I was a white knight, the man who rode to the rescue of those in need. I justified every decision, told myself that I believed in the

128

spirit of the law, if not always the letter. That I was the kind of man who could go places that the law never could.

Down these mean streets a man must walk, who is not himself mean . . .

But he is mean. As mean as those streets. Meaner, maybe. He couldn't survive if he wasn't. The world doesn't look kindly on the good and the just. It doesn't care.

Burns told me that we were the same.

I was beginning to realize that he was right.

Except that he had accepted who he was long ago. Learned to live with it. What separated us were what we cared about, the things we held in esteem. He cared for his family, for those close to him and for himself. I worried about other people, about those who were not mean enough to survive.

I would kill to protect them.

I had killed.

Forget the justifications I gave myself.

I killed to protect the innocent.

To avenge the dead.

Burns killed because it was convenient to do so.

And looking in my eyes, in that moment, Teale saw the truth. Understood who and what I was. That I was worse than he could ever hope to be. Because I had killed for what I believed. I hadn't murdered by accident or simply by not caring. I had killed for a purpose. A cause. And because of that, I could do it again.

He recoiled.

The pyromaniac – the man who didn't care

who he hurt, what he burned – recoiled from me in fear.

And I didn't care.

Twenty-Five

Gemma Fairstead.

Forty-three. Never married. Graduated with a degree in medicine, but never held down a job for long. Like she got itchy feet. Got bored.

A degree in medicine. Many psychopathic individuals have an interest in medicine or anatomy. Something to do with power, maybe. Many of them are highly intelligent. Power and knowledge. A good combination. So why did she never do anything with her education? Why not even an attempt at a normal life?

She had records from childhood. Sealed, of course. Could have been anything from shoplifting to assault. Clearly nothing serious enough to prevent her attempt at a medical career. But I had an idea what she'd been up to.

You can infer a lot about a person by the company they keep.

Pyromania starts early. There's a list of warning signs developmental psychologists are asked to watch for. But, like all psychotics, the specifics of pyromania vary from case to case. There's no age where you see the warning signs flashing on and off in neon. Taken on their own, several of the indicators are little more than normal adolescent angst. Sometimes, in figuring things out, kids can go a little crazy. A sealed record doesn't have to mean anything.

Except, of course, when it does.

Her previous address was a front. But I knew that already. To all intents and purposes, Gemma had vanished. Leaving behind a mess of false leads and unverifiable information. Only natural considering what she did for a living, the kind of people she worked for. And, of course, the number that Teale had used to contact her was no longer in service. I didn't have time to sweat the information out of him. Man like that would cave only so far and no further.

So how did I go about finding Gemma Fairstead? How did I find someone who didn't want to be found?

On my business cards, one of the quoted specialities was 'skip tracing'. Finding people who were deemed untraceable. Bad debts. Missing spouses. That kind of thing. If you covered your tracks, I could and would uncover them.

Officially, of course, it was all done through the correct legal channels. But sometimes you buck the system a little. In the name of expediency.

A good investigator requires a strong moral compass. You might bend the rules, but you have to know how not to break them completely. The News Group International trial brought that problem to the fore, when some of our number used the unofficial bag of tricks for investigations that were morally suspect. Just because you can do something doesn't always mean that you should.

But there are times when you do bad – or at least legally grey – things for the right reasons. I needed to find Gemma Fairstead. Talk to her. I already knew why she'd set the bomb. But I needed to hear it from her. I needed detail. More than hearsay and guesswork.

In the back of my mind, I was asking questions:

Who do you need to know for?

Yourself?

Or the old man?

David Burns. A man I considered repellent, less than human. And now, having seen him broken and vulnerable, was I looking to help him? To gain revenge on those who had struck at his family?

I had never been much of a sleeper, but now, at night, I slept less and less. The hours growing shorter. Often, I'd just lie there and stare at the ceiling, lost in my own doubts.

Wondering how I would be judged.

I always claimed to be an atheist, or at the very least, agnostic. But something about the old Catholicism that had come down through my grandparents still stuck with me. That sense that I was being constantly judged. Whatever I did, I would be punished for it.

God is always watching. Waiting for you to slip up.

Heaven is for the pure. For those who repent. But how can you repent when you're uncertain what your sins are? When you've done the wrong things for the right reasons?

Twenty-Six

'Where are you?'

Crossing the Tay Bridge and heading into Fife. But I wasn't about to tell Griggs. He could go hang for all I cared.

'Driving.'

'For him?'

'For myself.'

'I've got people breathing down my neck, McNee. They need answers. Results.'

'This could have ended long before now. You know that. Your bosses have to know it, too.'

'Aye, it could have. But not the right way.'

His constant refrain. The insistence was worrying. He didn't just want to see Burns behind bars. He wanted the old man to suffer. This was old-school justice. Did Griggs give a damn about the legality of his operation?

What had fuelled this obsession?

Griggs had crossed a lot of people in his time. He'd nearly been killed during the final days of the Kennedy brothers' reign in the city's east end; a long-held grudge spilling over and landing him in hospital. In those days, the old man had been keeping his head down, waiting to see the end of his rivals as their empire imploded. Griggs had never been involved in the investigations into Burns's activities, except on the periphery. They had no reason to deal with each other.

So what happened?

Was I asking the wrong questions? Looking in the wrong places?

In the bad old days I had been searching for surrogate bad guys: people I could blame for all the bad shite in the world. Maybe Griggs was the same, fixating all his anger on someone he had never really known, but who fit a certain profile.

Maybe that was it. But it didn't sit right. Didn't feel true.

'You have to trust me,' I said. 'Some things that I do . . .'

'I'm better off not knowing?'

'Deniability. It works for the old man, right?'

'Just remember why we're doing this.'

'Never leaves my mind.'

When I cleared the line, I was on the dual carriageway, heading deep into Fife. I turned off the main roads, on to winding country tracks. Flicked the headlights on full, illuminated the farmland before me. The crops cast long shadows.

I drove through small villages, past Guardbridge, hitting the oddly angled roundabout, taking the long way round to Cupar. Using the drive to clear my mind. The roads were quiet. Lambchop provided the soundtrack. The sound low, the music twisting in my brain.

Cupar's a small market town that's seen better days. Its home to one of Fife's biggest secondary schools, and while the council operates its offices from the town, there's a feeling like it's little more than a commuter base. Nothing ever happens. If you want quiet, it's the place to be.

I drove through the main artery, turned off at

the war memorial, tripped alongside the river Eden and out to a small estate on the edge of the town. New buildings. A hope for the future when they went up in the sixties, now they looked tired and ready for their end. Small, boxy bungalows. Lawns in various stages of trim. Some resolutely proud. Others despondently forgotten.

I found the house I wanted. Same as the rest on the outside. A beat-up looking Fiesta parked on the street. Second-hand or long cared for? Hard to say.

I walked to the front door. Someone was in. Light sliced out from behind the dark curtains that swung across the living room window.

I rang the bell. Waited.

When she answered, Gemma Fairstead had to fight not to do a double take. But for just a moment, her eyes went wide and the blood rushed from her cheeks. Maybe she had expected me to be dead along with the mark. Maybe she thought I'd never make the connection.

Maybe she just never thought about the consequences of her actions.

On that, at least, I could relate.

But she couldn't know why I was here. Not if she was to maintain the innocent act. She had to keep up the bluff she'd played the night we met.

I wasn't going to make it easy on her.

'It's late.'

'You don't remember me?'

'I . . . no. No, I don't.'

'Two nights ago, you were in Dundee. Round the back of Tay Mills, heading towards the clubs, I think. Liquid. Sams, maybe.'

'Right. Maybe.'

'We talked.'

'I had a wee bit to drink. But . . . I don't give out my telephone . . .'

'On the street. We met on the street.'

'I . . .'

'I was with a friend. He was a little the worse for wear.'

'I'm sorry. I hope he's feeling bett—'

'He's feeling dead.'

She licked her lips. You wouldn't see the sweat if you weren't looking for it. She could keep cool even after the initial shock. In her line of work she had to develop that skill. You work with incendiaries, you quickly learn the dangers that panic can bring. You suppress the natural instincts that come with fight or flight. If you don't, most likely, you die.

I used to know a guy worked bomb disposal for the army. Best poker player I ever knew. Because he could suppress his tics. Control his involuntary twitches. He had to. One wrong twitch on the job, he wouldn't have the hands to hold his cards.

It was the same thing with Gemma. Her obsession was dangerous. If she didn't respect that, she'd have been dead long ago. She had the cool, collected nature of someone accustomed to extreme pressure.

Talk about transferable skills.

'What happened? To your friend.' Like she didn't know. But I could have believed her if I allowed myself a moment of doubt.

'Let's talk inside,' I said.

'I don't know who you are.'

I pulled my wallet, showed her my ABI card. Of course I was no longer a member of the Association – they suspended my membership when the questions about my legal conduct were first raised, and while no one had officially made a statement, I assumed from the long silence that my suspension was probably a permanent expulsion – but I still had the ID, and most people wouldn't bother to check any further than that. It's the same phenomenon that allows you to walk in almost anywhere wearing a suit and carrying a clipboard. People are lazy enough to assume that if you look like who they think you are, there's no way that you could lie to them.

I had one more advantage as I talked my way through the front door of Gemma Fairstead's place: she was trying to appear normal. She was the one with something to hide; lying just as much to me as I was to her.

She wanted to be duped.

Just to appear normal.

Twenty-Seven

The house was decorated in neutral colours. Greys and creams. The front room had a shag carpet, a white leather sofa, matching recliners. A big screen TV in one corner played *The Xtra Factor* on low volume. The one that no one really watches unless they're obsessed, drunk, bored, or not that interested.

Which was she?

Judging by the CD racks on the wall, she wasn't a music fan: Tesco and Asda's idea of the top selling artists of all time dominated. Phil Collins. Meatloaf. Bonnie Tyler. A little Beyoncé to show her modern side. A bland kind of normalcy.

If there is one sign of a true sociopath, it's this: they will always have at least one Phil Collins album in their collection.

If they have more than one, chances are they've killed at least two people. Probably while listening to Phil. The only thing worse would be a Sting solo album.

I scanned the shelves more closely.

Check.

Gemma offered me a seat on the sofa beneath the window. I took it. Our eyes remained locked. Did she blink?

She sat on the other sofa, crossed her legs. Maybe trying for sexy, but the effect was neutered by her eyes. They looked at me with the kind of gaze a butterfly collector might reserve for their latest specimen right before it goes under the glass.

'Your friend was killed?'

'He was my client.'

'Oh?'

'There were a lot of people who might have wanted to harm him. I'm just . . .'

'He was a singer, then? Or actor? Didn't recognize him.'

'No, nothing like that.'

'Sounds juicy.'

'I want to talk to you about the night we met. Maybe you saw someone else hanging around?'

'Someone who could have killed your friend?' Her voice was carefully neutral. Her head moved forward. Made me think of a praying mantis. To become so detached takes a natural predisposition and a lot of practice.

'Yes, that's what I was thinking . . .'

She nodded. 'Sure you don't want a tea?'

'I'm fine.'

'Still, think I could do with one. Maybe with something a little stronger in there, too?'

I nodded. She stood up and walked to the door. She stopped, looked back at me over her shoulder. 'You never did say how you found out who I was . . .'

I didn't say anything. Let her leave.

Did she know that I knew? Was she going to make a run for it?

I waited for a moment. Then stood up. I checked those CDs again. Not wanting to appear too eager. We were playing Chicken. First one to give away the fact that they knew what the other was hiding was the loser.

After a few moments, I walked through to the back of the house. Slow and casual. She was filling the kettle. Perfectly ordinary. The kitchen was long, galley-style with clear glass-fronted cabinets and a table that folded out from the wall. The back door was at the far end, with a frosted glass porthole at head height.

Gemma said, 'You think I was going to make a run for it?'

'You know why I'm here?'

'You mean, dropping all the shite?'

'Yes.'

'You tell me.'

'You know who I am.'

'You're a lucky man, Mr McNee. Tell me why the police aren't outside. Tell me why they're not chapping on the door right now.'

'They don't know.'

'Is it true what they say about you?'

'Depends.'

'That you used to be one of the good guys. You were polis, and now you work for whoever pays the most?'

'I work for the people I choose to work for.'

'Not really an answer.'

'No, it's not.'

'Sure you don't want any tea? Or just the whisky?'

I shook my head.

She turned the kettle on. 'Tea's good for you. Relaxing. Nothing like it. Got to be good and milky, though. A touch of sugar when you're feeling indulgent. And, well, the other bit's optional . . .'

'I'm not interested in you,' I said. 'I'm interested in who hired you.'

'You were a professional investigator,' she said. 'Before they chucked you out of the Association.'

'You've done your homework.'

'They give me a job, I like to know what I'm up against. The preparation . . .'

'Is part of the thrill.'

'You get it, then?'

'Sure.'

And maybe I did. There was something to be said about the prep work on an investigation. Whether the case was as simple as a cheating spouse or more complex, such as a skip trace, it was the work you did before diving into the investigation that intrigued.

The foreplay.

And that was how she saw it. It was clear. She delighted in the lingering time before the main event. The fire and the explosion and the flames got her off, but the delay of the event was just as enticing in its own way.

She smiled. 'Once I tell you what you want to know, who's to say you won't just call the cops, anyway?'

'I have an honest face?'

'Maybe you did when you were younger. But you're getting lines, Mr McNee. Bags under the eyes. How do you sleep at night?'

'How do you sleep?'

'Would you like to find out?'

I shook my head.

'I could set your world on fire.'

'I bet you could.'

'So what happens now?'

'You tell me what I want to know.'

'And why would I do that?'

I smiled. 'Because if you don't talk to me, someone else will be here.'

'And what if you don't walk out of here?'

'Oh, we have an arrangement. You know who I work for. You know that the man you were hired to kill was his nephew. And you know what will happen if he ever finds out who you are. He won't care that someone paid you. He won't care that you didn't know who you were sent to murder.'

'So I tell you, and you call off the bloodhounds?'

'Something like that.'

She finished her tea. Lots of milk. No sugar. Sipped at it swiftly. Little pecks. A hummingbird grabbing pollen from a flower. 'Jesus,' she said. As though He could somehow help. 'Sophie's choice, eh?'

I didn't say a word.

Was this what I had become?

The man who judged others? The man who chose who got to have a choice and who didn't? A good man would have called the police and told them what he knew. Instead, I alienated the authorities and delivered my own justice. As though I didn't trust the police to follow through on their own remit.

I was a stubborn bastard. Because I believed my own bullshit. In my head, I was the white knight, the one person who could make the world better. Who could wade through the sewage of the world and rescue the things worth saving. The flotsam and jetsam of decency and morality.

The white knight can do no wrong. Sometimes you have to do the wrong things for the right reasons. Those were the lessons I had learned from movies in the eighties when I was growing up. You can kill the bad guys and everything will still be all right because they were bad and you were good. Anyone can do anything for the right reasons.

I had got away with it once.

Twice, in fact.

Now I believed in my own immunity.

But did that still make me one of the good guys?

Gemma Fairstead had killed a man. Not a pleasant man, but not a monster either. Just someone with a confidence issue and an impossible need to live up to the reputation of his uncle. She had killed before. I was sure of it. She may not have explicitly admitted to it, but she wanted to. Just beneath that calm exterior, the pride at what she'd done scrabbled to burst out and announce itself to the world. Like the alien in the Ridley Scott movies.

Regardless of what she had done, who she had hurt, did I have any right to threaten her? Did I have any right to judge her with no one else to witness my decision?

The ABI had suspended me under suspicion of breaking the ethical code of the association. Had I taken this as a licence to become a vigilante?

I said, 'This is your decision. Just tell me how to find Craig Nairn.'

She smiled. 'You knew his name all along?'

Sometimes you go fishing when you just think there's a shark in the water. 'Never start an interview where you don't know the answers you're looking for.'

'You're good.' She smiled, but behind those

eyes I couldn't be sure if she wasn't mocking me.

'A telephone number . . . an address . . .'

'So . . . you send the heavies after him instead of me?'

'Do you really care?'

She was the gun. She wasn't pulling the trigger. She was a psychopath, no question, and maybe if she hadn't killed Robert Burns, she would have killed someone else. But it was her nature. Burns wanted someone to blame. And that person, ultimately, was Craig Nairn. The man who wanted to topple the old monarch and become the new king.

Part of me would have left them to settle their own private war. But I was in the middle of it, now. No turning back. No getting out.

I had started this. I would finish it, too.

'Just tell me where to find him.'

'There's a number I called. All I had. These things, they don't work by just picking a number out of the Yellow Pages.'

'But you knew who he was?'

'He didn't tell me his name, but I figure it's the same man. Be a coincidence if two men wanted your friend dead for different reasons.'

Maybe not. But I didn't say anything.

She wrote the number on the back of a kitchen roll. I put it in my pocket. 'Thank you.'

'What happens now?'

'To you?'

'Yes.'

'Whatever you like.'

She didn't trust me. Had no reason to. I could

144

have called Burns and told him that she was here. She might have given me what I wanted, but that meant she was no longer useful to me. Why should I care? Just because she was the gun and not the person pulling the trigger wouldn't really make any difference to David Burns. He'd want her and Nairn dead. He'd want Nairn's family dead. Everyone the man had ever known. Because in his head, that would be the only thing that could cancel out the blood-soaked tragedy of his nephew's murder.

But would it make a difference?

Any of it?

I turned to go.

The glass on the kitchen door shattered.

I turned. Two men barged through. Heavy-set. Dark clothes. Knit hats. Rough faces. I didn't recognize them. One of them grabbed Gemma, knocked her legs out from under her. She fell to the ground.

The other came at me. I tried to sidestep him, but the kitchen was too narrow. He punched low, caught me in the stomach with his fist. A meat sledgehammer. Knocked the wind out of me. Nearly knocked my lunch out, too.

I doubled over. He grabbed my hair, pulled my head back. I went on my knees. Slow. He kept up the pressure.

'Don't make this any worse than it has to be,' he said. 'We're here for her. But you, pal, you're just an added bonus.'

Twenty-Eight

The blindfold came off. I blinked. The world forced itself into focus. Purple and grey spots bounced around like blobs of wax in a lava lamp. Shapes slowly formed an odd coherence.

I blinked again.

The room was small. Dull walls. Unvarnished floorboards. You wouldn't walk around barefoot. A bare bulb in the ceiling, its wiring exposed at the root, cast a harsh light. I had been placed in a plastic bucket chair. Made me think of school; long, hot afternoons in a class that never ended. I didn't want to think about what lessons they might want to teach me here.

A man stood before me, arms crossed. Trying to look like he meant business. Except his forehead was gently sweating and you could see his fingers twitching. This was not a natural hardman. This was a wannabe. He was about twenty-five or twenty-six years old, dressed in blue jeans and a black T-shirt with the white Nike swoop on the left side.

'Awright, Slick.'

I said, 'Craig Nairn?'

He nodded. 'Mr McNee.'

'Showing respect,' I said. 'Good move. Pity you didn't think of that earlier.'

He shook his head. 'You're a pain in the arse, you know that?'

146

'It's been said. By better than you.'

'Funny man, too. Great. Been a while since I've talked to a funny man.' He leaned forward. 'Know what I do to funny men?'

'Write them a cheque and send them on their way?'

He turned away from me. I tried to look round the room again, get a better sense of where I was. Might have once been an office. Maybe we were in an old garage or office block on an industrial estate. Or just a back room somewhere. Hard to say. The details were too anonymous. The room too enclosed. As though nothing existed beyond its four walls.

All I could say for certain was that there was no way I was going to get a punch in with Mr Nairn. Not with the two bruisers from Gemma Fairstead's kitchen standing on either side of me.

We'd arrived by car. Leather seats. Quiet engine. Good driver, too. The turns had been smooth, barely noticeable. Out of the car, they walked me up steps. We had gone inside. I could tell by the echoes of noise around me that we were in an enclosed space. Gave up counting around thirty-two steps. The steps had been uneven. My guide had practically dragged me up them. Part of the reason I lost count. What all this told me was simple: this building was old. Out of the way. Empty. Maybe not even within the city limits.

Nairn said, 'You're in over your head, Slick. But you did your best to save the life of my . . . friends . . . That cunt Gaske was the one who killed them. So I'm offering you the chance to

147

walk away. Now. With your life. This has nothing to do with you. No need to worry about whatever it is the old bastard's holding over your head.' He leaned in. 'Because no one works for him willingly. Am I right?'

'Care to tell me why?'

'Why I'd let you live?'

'I'm not as smart as I look.'

'Don't piss me about, McNee. That kind of shite might work with the old man, but I'm all about business. Keep It Simple, Stupid.' He seemed to have a bit of trouble remembering the acronym. Like someone else had taught it to him. His speech had the air of having been written by someone else. The words sounded unnatural coming out of his mouth, like an accented computer reciting words learned by rote. The sounds were there, but the intention was missing.

'Meaning?'

'The goal is the thing. You get there by any means necessary.'

'Including killing innocents?'

'Robert Burns wasn't innocent.'

'He wasn't part of your war with the old man.'

'He was the old man's blood. Killing him got the fucking message over, aye?'

I'm not sure Nairn knew the kind of message he'd really sent.

'And Gemma Fairstead?'

'She . . . came highly recommended . . .' He hesitated. Wouldn't turn to look at me. But something in his stance gave away his nerves. He was talking the talk, but didn't seem like he could walk the walk. Didn't have the spine for it.

Made me wonder if he really was as deadly as the old man thought. Or if this was all an act. He didn't seem like a criminal mastermind on paper. In real life the effect was dulled even further. I had the feeling that the two hard men on either side of me would eat Nairn for their breakfast.

What was his secret?

'But . . .?' I needed him to open up. He was questioning me, but I knew I could turn it round, get some answers of my own.

For all the good it would do me.

The chances of me walking out of this room alive were slim. Even if I did agree to Nairn's terms. Whoever was pulling his strings probably didn't want a loose end out there to be tugged on. And I would be a very loose string indeed.

'But . . .' Nairn hesitated. Either forgetting what he was going to say or going for dramatic effect. He turned, gave me the full on evil-bastard look. But it was a child playing at evil. The squinty-eyes. The attitude-adjust in the shoulders. But I'd met enough evil bastards in my time to know when someone was play-acting. In his own way, Nairn was like Robert – don't call me Rabbie – Burns. A wee boy playing in the big lad's playground.

He said, 'She knew too much. Sooner or later Burns would make the connection. He's got the nous.'

'He's got me. It wasn't tough finding her.'

He wasn't about to let me get in the way of his little game. He had something to say.

149

Something he'd been told to say. And he was going to say it. No deviations. No improvisations. 'And before he killed her, he'd make sure she gave him my name.'

No, this didn't make sense at all. Craig Nairn was saying all the right things. Just not in the right tone of voice.

Who was he? Really?

'And what about me?' I asked.

'You're going to deliver a message to David Burns.'

'Aye? And what's that?'

'No one is safe, Mr McNee. No one. The old man's days are done. He's faded. Past it. Clapped out. Fucked.'

'You're the new king of the world?'

'That's the one.'

The bruiser on my left moved behind the chair. He pinned my arms. Held me down. The other one moved in front of me. Grinned.

I knew what was coming.

Tried to relax. The more you tense yourself, the worse it hurts.

Twenty-Nine

Driving home, I pulled over twice. Falling out of the car in my rush to vomit at the side of the road. Tasting blood every time.

My insides ached when I breathed too deep or shifted my weight. When I caught sight of myself

150

in the rear view, I thought of the monster from the Frankenstein novels: cracked flesh and dried blood.

Going over the bridge, I blanked twice. Found myself close to the edge, shaving the barriers. The car weaved between lanes. Any traffic cop would have pulled me over, but the worst I got was horn-blasts from other road users.

I pulled up outside the flat, hauled myself upstairs. Nearly collapsed in the hall. I made it to the bedroom, fell on to the sheets and closed my eyes.

I think I dreamt.

About pain and guilt and foolish mistakes. Fire and smoke and fear. Maybe it was only a preview of what was to come. An early glimpse of hell. Because even though I was lapsed, part of me still believed strongly enough that I could wind up there.

Through the best of intentions, of course.

I woke up. Muscles stretched and aching, face thrumming like a bass amplifier at a jazz concert. My vision was bright around the edges, as though light was coming out from under my eyelids. The aftertaste of blood and vomit lingered in my mouth. The scent of sick and sweat lightly teased my nostrils. I rolled and tried to stand. Ended up back on the bed, chest tight and head empty, as though my brains had leaked out during the beating.

But I finally stood up and made my way to the bathroom. Leaned against the sink and gulped in air, unable to look straight on at my reflection.

Nairn had told he was using me to send Burns a message.

The message was this:

I can be merciful.

He'd whispered that to me as I lay on the floor of that bare room, curled in on myself, body quaking with pain.

I managed to shower and went to the living room. I turned on the TV to STV news. The newscaster finished a story about Alex Salmond's latest pledge for an independent Scotland.

Then, the sombre face: 'A Fife woman died late yesterday evening in a house fire in Cupar, Fife. The woman – forty-three-year-old Gemma Fairstead – did not escape the blaze that spread to neighbours' houses. No one else was injured during the incident. Police and fire officers are unsure how the fire started, but believe that it may have been set deliberately . . .'

That got me moving. The adrenaline pushing past the aches and pains. I stumbled into the bedroom, found my jacket where I'd left it on the floor. Found the mobile still intact in the inside pocket.

'Where the fuck've you been?'

'I met your man Nairn.'

'Oh, aye?'

'He had a message for you.'

'Care to share.'

'I think it's the kind of thing we should talk about in person.'

Thirty

'Let him sit down, David.' When I'd met her a few years earlier, Burns's wife had treated me as though I was the devil himself. Over the past few months, she had come to think of me more softly. Seeing what she believed to be another side to me. The same way she had perhaps softened to Ernie, too, the man who had harassed her husband so many times on official police business, and yet became a family friend, a dinner guest, a confidant. When I gave the old man a lift to meetings, Mary Burns would greet me with black coffee and insist I sit at the breakfast bar while Burns finished whatever it was that had distracted him that morning. Now she was fussing over me, the concern etched into her features. I'd seen her look this way before when she thought her husband had been harmed during an attempt on his life.

Funny how things can change.

Funny how I only felt guilt over my deception when I had the distance to think about it.

'You OK to stand, son?'

'Aye.'

'Then let him alone,' the old man said to Mary. 'We need to have a wee word in private.'

We walked out to the back garden. Stood down the far end, near the fence that backed on to scrubland, and, beyond that, the railway that led to Aberdeen and all points north. Burns said, 'Tell me.'

I told him what I knew. Leaving out that I had offered Gemma Fairstead the chance to escape. Fudging my motivations for seeking her out. I had simply been trying to confirm the facts before approaching him. His time, after all, was precious. Didn't want to waste it.

His response was simple: 'Dangerous move.'

I nodded. He was right in more ways than he suspected.

Burns reached into his pocket, pulled out a pack of cigarettes. 'I quit. So she thinks. But at my age, what's the worst that can happen?' He offered me one. I almost took it, but withdrew my hand at the last second, shaking my head.

We stood in silence for a while. Burns said, 'He was a chancer. Always was. But something like this . . .'

'Not his style.'

'He's too fucking dumb. You can say it. I'm being kicked around by a fucking mental midget.'

There was that. And nothing I had seen proved otherwise. Burns hadn't underestimated Craig Nairn. But there was something that we had been missing this whole time. And perhaps the only person who could answer our questions was Nairn himself.

'So what do we do?'

'You get some bedrest. Jesus, look at you. Bloody sight, you are, son.'

'And you?'

He didn't answer me. Looked across at the tracks. Had he ever considered just walking away

154

from it all? He made a big deal about being a self-made man. Working his way up from nothing. I always wondered if he really believed that the sacrifices he made had been worthwhile. He had let go of normality and security to gain wealth and power. But with that came the constant threat of someone like Nairn who thought that he could take it all away from Burns, who thought that he could inherit that wealth and power.

There was always one.

Burns had taken it from his predecessors, of course. The Kennedys had been the city's dominant crime family for decades. Burns had been an enforcer for the old man, passing down his empire to his two sons. When the elder Kennedy died, Burns struck out on his own, knowing that the two lads were too much in love with the product that they supplied to last long in the business. Their empire and influence slowly shrunk. Eight years ago, the brothers had been murdered – executed – in a case that the police never solved. But there were rumours. There are always rumours.

That new swimming pool down by Riverside had very strong foundations.

'I can help you.'

'You're not able to do what needs to be done. I've always known that about you, son. You're flexible. But every man has a point where they break. I don't think you've found yours yet. But I know where it is.'

He knew about the man I had killed six years earlier. He knew that I'd willingly delivered another to his death. But perhaps he thought those were the exceptions that proved the rule. Or that killing another man would irredeemably change me. Or that the context had to be right for me to act. I couldn't justify the deaths of faceless others in a war over drugs and territory the same way that I could justify the death of those who had inflicted pain and suffering on innocents.

I'd always believed that Burns hid himself from the moral quandaries of his life. But the more time I spent with him, the more I realized that he truly understood who and what he was. He just chose to ignore the moral problems such duality posed.

What's worse?

To become a monster and never accept that fact?

Or live every day with the monster that you created?

Burns looked at me for a moment, side-on. Maybe reassessing, trying to decide whether he had misjudged me. 'You're in no state, either way. So here's the thing. This wee bollock's coming after me and my family. He's made that much clear. My wife . . . she knows who I am, even if she doesn't know everything. She's been with me through it all. The court cases, the raids, the wars, the good times, the bad times, all of it. When they've banged me up on suspicion, she's the one comes every time bail me out and never says a fucking word. She means everything to me, McNee.'

I'd already let him down once. And here he was again asking me to protect his family. Was his confidence in me that strong? Or was this another attempt to keep me on the sidelines? Another babysitting job? One that he felt I couldn't possibly fuck up.

It was hard to tell. The old man was an accomplished liar. The only way you could see the truth of him was in his actions. And by then it was often too late. As too many corpses could attest.

I hesitated.

'You're the one who came to me,' he said. 'Offered your support. Your allegiance.'

'Because I had no other choice.'

He nodded. 'Keep telling yourself that. You were cast out from your old friends. Oh, it's a tragedy, all right, son. The good man who did all the wrong things for the right reasons.' Was he mocking me? It was hard to tell. There was a bitterness dancing just underneath the words.

'Isn't that how you see yourself?'

'Like I said, we're more alike than you might care to admit.'

What could I say to that?

'She's an innocent, McNee.'

Really? Perhaps, in our world, innocence was simply a matter of degrees. But I had to wonder if his wife – who knew and quietly accepted the truth about her husband – was still complicit in his guilt.

'You told me once that all you wanted was to do the right thing. This is the right thing, McNee. Protecting someone who has done nothing wrong.'

'And what about you?'

'I'll pay for my sins. Sooner or later. All of them. The reckoning comes to us all in the end.

So they tell us every fucking Sunday. I accepted that a long time ago.'

Did that make it easier or harder for him, I wondered? To know that the end, when it came, would be a tally of all his willingly accepted evils?

Thirty-One

She knew why I was there. She didn't like it.

Neither of us said anything, however. Just tried to carry on like everything was normal. She showed me the TV in the front room, told me that they had the full Sky Package. Anything I wanted to watch, I could. Except the blue channels, of course. Not that I looked like the kind of man who'd be into that.

I surfed for a while, stuck with BBC News 24. Watched as they tried their best to spin out stories that had stalled hours earlier. The news, like any good story, relies not on the moments between, but on the relative seconds of action that capture us. Good news is real life with the boring parts snipped out.

But in our all-day-all-night society, we get to relive the boring moments, too. Allowing ourselves to understand the frustration that comes with waiting for something – anything – to happen. For those watching, did that make the drama more or less involving? I really had to wonder.

Mary Burns busied herself in the kitchen. I

heard her rattling about in cupboards. Realized that beyond her devotion to her husband, I knew nothing about who she was, where she had grown up, how she really felt. All I had to go on were the impressions filtered through the old man's talk of her.

I tried to watch the news, but I couldn't relax. Kept looking at the door every time she walked by.

I tried not to think about it. Distracted myself. Looked at the mantelpiece. Saw the family photos. Stood up and moved closer. The records of a family down the years. A young looking Burns and Mary standing outside their home, maybe after having bought it for the first time. She was already pregnant, beginning to show, looking proud as she cupped her stomach with both hands, while he beamed with a paternal air, arm draped across her shoulders to hold her close. There were pictures of the children as they grew up. All three of them – two girls and a boy. None of them lived at home, now. They had all moved out as soon as possible. One of the girls didn't even correspond with her father any more, lived with her husband somewhere in California and pretended her family had died when she was a girl. I doubted it had anything to do with a lack of love from her parents. But I had to wonder about the sense of betrayal she might have felt when she realized the truth about what her father did to earn the money that kept them in food, clothes and education.

It was clear that the family home had been a loving place when she was growing up. You can't fake a certain kind of smile. And in every picture, the kids were happy, their parents proud. They were the ideal family. Just don't think about how they got that way.

The children disappeared in their early twenties. There were a few pictures of grandchildren, but the parents were noticeably absent in each.

What price had Burns really paid for the power he had built over the years?

The next time Mary walked past, I opened the door and said, 'What was his name? The lab, I mean.' In the pictures taken from years ago, when their children were young, when her hair had been long and tumbled over unblemished skin, there was a dog that stood beside them. A black Labrador. Proud and faithful. Dogs are simple animals at heart. You can tell a lot just by looking at them. This one had been a real family pet. Devoted. Faithful. Loved.

'His name was Glen.' Her face softened, and I saw something of the young woman in the photographs. 'We got him just after the first wean was born, you know? He used to sit guard over Andy every night. Watch him sleep, as though afraid the wee one would just suffocate. Same with the girls, too.' She bit her lower lip. 'Bloody lovely dog.'

'What happened?'

'He got old.'

'I'm sorry.'

'He had a good life. You like dogs?'

I nodded.

'Come with me,' she said.

We went to the second level of the house. Up

the narrow stairs. Past the bedroom to what I had always assumed was just a box or spare room. She opened the door, and walked inside. I followed her. The sharp smell of paint caught me.

The room was filled with paintings of dogs. Still lives. Observed moments. Thick oil based paints on tough canvases. A real attention to detail. Especially around the eyes. She had a way of capturing a dog's eyes, of giving you a sense that in the moment of creation she understood what her subjects were really thinking.

I didn't know much about art. But that didn't stop me from understanding talent. The only person whose work I had seen before that affected me upon viewing had been dead a few days later, her brains battered out by a bearded psychopath.

Funny the connections you make.

Funny how I always found myself thinking back on tragedies and loss.

I looked at the painting still on the canvas. Close up on a black lab; sad brown eyes staring soulfully out at the viewer. Not an internal kind of sadness. But an empathetic kind of stare, as though he could see through to what you were thinking. He wanted you to know that he understood your pain.

Then again, they say that people read into art what they bring with them.

'Beautiful,' I said.

'Just a hobby.'

'You could sell these,' I said. 'I know people. Café's, that kind of thing . . . they'd have people willing to—'

'No,' she said. Too quickly. 'No, it's just a hobby. I just thought you'd like them. You know, if you liked dogs.' Her voice trailed off, as though suddenly embarrassed at having let me see the pictures.

I turned to look at her. 'They're good. Did you train?'

She shook her head. 'Just a hobby. Helps me relax. Pass the time of day.'

'Does David know?'

'He knows. But I don't let him see them.'

'You should. He'd be proud.'

'He would always be proud,' she said, a little sadly. 'That's how he is.' As though she knew that pride was her husband's default setting. Even if he felt differently, he'd never really show it.

We were silent for a while. I looked at the pictures. Wondered how her life might have been if she never met David Burns. He loved her, I knew that. But his desire to protect her from the world had meant that she barely left the house without being accompanied by someone. There was a reason he'd left me behind with her. It wasn't to do with keeping me out of the loop. It was because he was genuinely afraid for her. He wanted someone with her. Someone who could stand in for him. Who could make sure that she was safe.

His greatest fear had always been that his personal life and his other interests would overlap. It wasn't just the fear of them being caught up in a media glare if he were to be arrested. It was the idea that someone looking to hurt him would hurt them.

So now, we were hitting the mattresses. The old man covering every angle. He knew what his enemy was capable of, now. He would do whatever it took to protect his family.

I admired that in a way.

But the admiration left me wondering, who was I working for any more?

Myself?

The old man?

Griggs?

We went back downstairs, to the kitchen. Sat at the breakfast bar and talked for a while. I drank coffee from the pot she kept hot all day. She told me about the man she married, how he had come into her life with a benevolent charm and the kind of chivalry she'd only ever read about in books. 'He was my hero. Stepping in at the dancing when I was being bothered by Bill Kirkton. The wee lech trying to cop a feel. I was too young to fight back properly and David just stepped in, laid a hand on Bill's shoulder, whispered something in his ear. You know, David didn't even try and kiss me until our third date.' She smiled softly at this, her eyes gaining the sheen of youth, as though the very act of remembering had wiped all the years and worries away, transformed her into the innocent girl she remembered being.

He was her protector. Her saviour. While to others he would become a monster, to Mary Burns, he would always be her gentle David.

I had to press. Couldn't help myself: 'But you know what he does. You've always known the things he had to do to get where he is.'

'People always knew what they were getting into. My David's an honest man, Mr McNee. In the same way I think you are. He would never

163

hurt anyone who didn't understand why. No one went into business with him blind.'

'And that makes it OK?'

'Are you a religious man?'

'Not really. I might have been a religious boy, but maybe that was just because people kept telling me to believe in God.'

'Maybe you should come back to the Church sometime. David always said you were a lost soul. Someone looking for a purpose in life. Maybe that's why he likes you. Even when you say such terrible things about him.' She sipped at her tea, eyes never leaving my face. I felt as though when she looked at me, she was expecting me to say something. But I didn't know what she wanted to hear. An apology? An acknowledgement that I had been wrong?

The silence between us stretched.

A car pulled up outside.

Burns back already?

I doubted it. He would be gone for days. Leaving me out of the loop.

So who?

I stood up, gestured for Mary to stay where she was. She looked ready to ask a question. But I was already moving.

Thirty-Two

Close protection is about trusting your own paranoia. See something, say something becomes the rule. You let yourself believe the worst can happen because then you're prepared when it actually does.

I went to the front room, kept myself to the side of the windows. Looked out at the street. Grey BMW. Four men climbing out. Didn't look like business types. They opened the front gate. I went back to the kitchen, hustled Mary into moving. She did so reluctantly. Not understanding my sudden change in attitude.

'My coat,' she said.

'We'll get it later,' I said. 'Just move . . .'

The knock came at the front door as I was opening the back. We bolted into the back garden. The space was blocked off, the only way out through the garage or back the way we came.

The second rule of close protection is preparation: always know your space. Always know the exits. I fished the garage keys from my pocket. Found myself wishing I'd taken up Burns on his offer of a weapon.

But what good would that do? Last time I'd used a gun, a man had died. I'd never really got past that, despite my posturing.

The key stuck in the lock. I twisted and rattled. Paused. Took a breath. Turned and clicked.

'Out the back!'

I didn't even look round to see how close the voice was. Just shoved Mary in ahead of me, and then locked the door behind us.

The front door of the garage led out into an alley between the houses. Burns's pride and joy – a restored Bentley with walnut panelling and burnt red bodywork – sat inside the small brick structure, covered up with a white cloth. No keys, of course. The old man wouldn't trust just anyone with this car.

Only one thing to do. I opened the front door, pulled the roller up. 'We're going to run,' I said. 'Next door. We're going to lock ourselves in and we're going to call someone I know.'

'Who?'

I had a few ideas.

We dashed down the alley. Way I figured it, the intruders were behind us, in the back yard. It would take them a few moments to work out what we'd done and by then we'd be barricaded in someone else's house. These guys didn't want to make a scene or hang around too long. Someone would call the police. Or worse.

I pushed Mary in front, to make sure that I had my eyes on her at all times. She was slow and unsteady. Not just age but fright. I moved just behind her, urging her forward. Conscious of how slow we were; certain that we weren't fast enough, that at any moment a hand would land on my shoulder, a blade would pierce my kidneys.

I'd been stabbed before. Had the scars to prove it. Not an experience I was eager to repeat.

We made it to the next house down, hammered hard. I shouldered the door when it started to open, pushing aside a man in his fifties. He protested in half-words and syllables that made no sense.

'Lock the door,' I told him. He did so, then looked at me with his eyes wide and his jaw dropped.

I ignored his hurt pride, and walked quickly to the rear of the house, pulling out my phone and swapping sim cards.

Susan answered in three rings.

'Unmarked,' I said. 'Safe house. Now.' I rattled off the address.

'Just you?'

'Mary Burns.'

'Oh, Jesus, Steed. What the fuck have you done?'

'You're not the one who's going to have to explain this to the old man.'

I was through with being somebody else's pawn.

I was ready to change the rules.

Thirty-Three

We waited it out in a bedroom upstairs. Sitting on the floor, far side of a king size bed. Like little kids in their parent's bedroom. Mary looked almost relaxed.

She said, 'This was always going to happen.'

'Maybe,' I said. 'Your husband has a lot of enemies.'

'It's what he always talked about. They would come after his family. They would come after me. They would come after the kids.' The emphasis on 'they' every time. The royal 'they'.

'And you?'

'What?'

'What were you scared of?'

'That they'd come after him.' She let her head roll back, looked up at the ceiling. 'What must you think of me? A silly old girl in love with a bad boy?'

'Less of the silly.'

'It's true, though. I know who he is, Mr McNee. What he does to people. I'm not a complete fool.'

'And?'

'And I see everything else about him. He's a loving father. He's a good husband.'

'You never showed him your paintings.'

'Every relationship needs boundaries. Are you married?'

I showed her naked fingers. Wiggled them. Got a smile.

'No girl, then?' She hesitated. 'Or boy?'

'No one,' I said. 'Not now.'

'There was that pretty policewoman, wasn't there? Ernie's lass?'

'Yes,' I said. 'For a while.'

'What happened?'

I almost said, *your husband*, and then held the thought. Not because it would upset her, but because it wasn't really true. He was just an easy target. Instead I said, 'Life.'

'You messed it up.' No blame in her voice. But she knew.

'We both did.' Because we didn't talk. About the important things. Because we tried to pretend that things were perfect when they weren't.

Maybe that was what she had been talking about when it came to her husband. She accepted who he was, no matter how ugly, and she talked

168

to him about it. There was no hiding, pretending it wasn't true.

Susan and I had hidden truths from each other that had been self-evident. We never talked about the things we knew we had done, about the blood that bound us together.

In the end, that silence was what drove us apart. Would we have been closer if we had talked about it? Could we have done things differently?

'Maybe there's still hope?'

'Maybe,' I said.

'How long do you think until your friends arrive?'

I didn't answer that.

Downstairs, someone was hammering on the door. Loud. Angry. I thought of those four beats from Beethoven: death knocking at the door.

Our host crawled in from the room across the hall. Pale. Shaking. 'This was supposed to be the safest street in the city.' He spoke in a loud whisper. 'When we bought . . . They said . . . Oh, Jesus . . . Your bloody husband . . .'

'You didn't complain when he found your fucking car last year.'

Our host stayed quiet. No smart-arse comeback to that.

'Or when he got you that whisky cut-price. Oh-no, no complaints there, eh, Jim?'

I looked at Mary. Surprised at the anger in her voice. She had always seemed so quiet, so mild, so accepting. To see genuine anger erupt from her was unexpected.

'And don't think I don't know how you look at us when we leave the house, or that I don't

169

see you at the window when the police cars come up. Don't think I don't bloody well know you were judging us. At the same time as you were using us. Pretending to be our friend. All for the thrill of knowing a gangster. Oh, aye, bet that made you feel like a man. A real man, eh, Jim?' She leaned forward. 'Still taking those pills? Annie says they don't really make that much difference. But she likes to pretend, eh?'

The man, on all fours, looked like a dog who'd been caught pissing behind the couch.

Downstairs, the hammering stopped. The noise had merely been a prelude. The real show was about to begin.

I said, 'Do you have a loft?'

'Yes.'

'Take her up there.'

'But . . .'

'Do it!'

He and Mary went into the hall. Keeping low, so their heads didn't appear above the line of the window-sills from outside. The man – Jim – pulled down the loft hatch and the extendable ladder. Climbed up first, of course. His own safety above that of an older woman.

Mary followed. Crouching in the cramped space above, she turned to look down at me. 'Come on, then?'

I shook my head. Folded the ladder and pushed the hatch shut again. Mary's mouth opened to say something, but I didn't listen.

I took a breath, stood up straight, walked down the stairs. Calm as you like.

The glass on the front door shattered. An arm

reached in, undid the lock from inside. I waited at the bottom of the stairs.

Special delivery.

The lead thug said, 'Where the fuck is she?'

I stood my ground.

'Give her up, you won't get hurt.'

Aye. Right.

Four of them. They spilled in the narrow hallway. I couldn't fight. Couldn't win. Not even if there had just been one of them. Check the shoulders, the thick necks, the tattooed forearms. The original heavies right there.

How long could I hold out?

How long before they figured they could just steamroller past me?

I figured there were worse ways for things to end.

On the street, a car engine roared and cut. Car doors slammed,

The thugs turned.

Voices yelled. 'On the ground. On the fucking ground!'

I made a dash for it, up the stairs. No point hanging around. One of the fuckers tried to follow. I turned, gripped the bannister, steadied myself against the wall and kicked out. Got him in the face with the heel of my boot. He fell back, toppled arse over tit and twisted badly as he fell. The wooden bannister couldn't take the strain, cracked and buckled as he slammed against it on his way down.

Six plainclothes. Not announcing themselves as coppers. Playing hard men to the hilt. The thugs probably figured them for Burns's men.

Way they dived in, they seemed to be enjoying the rammie.

Aye, well. Most police work is dull. Does everyone good to cut loose once in a while.

I could have helped. Maybe should have.

But the truth was, I wouldn't have been any use. I'd just have got in the way.

Story of my life.

Thirty-Four

Susan drove us west.

Beside me, in the back seat, Mary said, 'I thought you said you didn't talk anymore.' A little teasing in her tone, but it was strained. She was still processing what had happened.

'I try,' Susan said. Watching us in the rear view. Mary Burns looked out of the window at the city passing by. All of us trying to think about anything except where we were going and why.

'What will you tell your husband?' I asked.

Bringing her back to reality. We couldn't keep talking around the situation. 'Be straight with me. Are you working with the police?'

'It's more complex than that.'

'It always is.' The bitter voice of someone who's been betrayed before. And of course she had. By Ernie.

'Steed isn't working for us, Mrs Burns,' Susan said. 'He called me because we're friends. Because he needed someone he could trust. Right

172

now, given your situation, what you need is to be with someone who isn't caught up in the middle of your husband's war. He's too close. I'm not. My people are not.'

Mary Burns didn't say anything.

The safe house was in Birkhill, north west of the City. A small bungalow with subtly enhanced security measures, including enforced doors and a secure entry system. The back garden was enclosed by thick hedges, making it tough to launch a rear assault. Susan and I stood just outside the re-enforced French windows to the rear of the property. I was aching for a cigarette. Funny the cravings you get when you think how close you came to death. Most people would expect they might need a good, stiff drink.

I said, 'Thanks for lying.'

'Think she bought it?'

'She's tough to read.'

'Dad always said he could never understand why she was so devoted to the old man.'

'He has another side to him.'

'Oh?'

'Everyone does. Even the worst monsters in this world are kind to someone.'

'Is that a note of optimism?'

'I'm not sure that's really an optimistic thought.'

Susan nodded. 'Like Hitler being a vegetarian.'

We stood there in silence for a while.

I said, 'I'm worried about Griggs.'

'Aye?'

'The obsession.'

'He should have pulled you from service. He should have put an end to the operation months ago. This is out of control.'

'And why hasn't he? Pulled me? Ended this madness?'

'I don't know. Steed . . . I've been asking around . . . quiet, like. But . . . no one . . . there's no record of this operation. I'm supposed to be assigned to some other case under his authority. But as far as I can see, Sandy has been filing false reports. Giving updates that bear no relation to what he's actually doing. I just . . .'

I didn't know what to say.

'Steed, Sandy hasn't informed anyone about this project, about your working undercover. There are no records of an informant in Burns's gang since my father died. There's no funding. My father's death effectively ended the operation. He's been diverting cash from other projects. I've seen the records. I just . . .'

'You just don't know what to do?' They had been sleeping together. She had been compromised by personal involvement. I could understand.

'I care for him. He's a driven man.'

'You haven't learned by now? About driven men?'

She forced a smile. 'My father. Always was a daddy's girl.'

'So there's no record that I was coerced into this situation?'

'No.'

'And there's no funding for an op against the old man?'

'Not any more.'

'So why? What's in this for Griggs?'

She shook her head.

Neither of us could answer the question.

All we could do was react to what we now knew. Try and figure a way to resolve the mess we were in.

And hope to hell it wouldn't get us killed.

Thirty-Five

'So she's safe?'

I nodded. The old man, in the passenger seat, seemed happy with that answer.

'She's with people I trust.'

'Then I trust them.' No doubt in his voice. If I even thought about betraying him, I knew the consequences. So he trusted me. Because I would have to be stupid to try and pull the wool over his eyes.

Lucky he didn't know me as well as he thought he did.

'He's a slippery little bastard,' Burns said. Meaning Craig Nairn. 'No one seems to know where the fuck he is.'

'Our new friend might.'

'You might be right, son. Even a fucked clock's right twice a day, eh?'

We pulled up outside the old hotel. City centre location. Across from the rail station, prime views of the river. The building was closed.

Had been empty for over a decade before that. When it reopened, the plan was for it to be a premier destination for the new Dundee. There was talk of the city applying for City of Culture status for 2017. The hotel was part of the planning stage. With the V&A coming to the city and a virtual regeneration of the waterfront already underway, the new Dundee was to be an aspirational and shining beacon for Scotland's future.

But the foundations were only just being laid.

And as with any foundation, there were bound to be a few bodies hidden in the darker recesses.

Burns had a skeleton key for the building. He'd called ahead, turned off the security cameras. There would be no record of what happened.

Inside, you could see something of what the building had once been: the grand sweeping staircase, the expansive lobby, and the chandelier fittings in the high ceiling. But there was a sense of abandonment, too. The dust motes that danced in the light of torches. The odd stillness punctuated by the occasional creak from contracting old boards.

We climbed the staircase to the third floor. I thought of *The Shining*. The long and endless corridors of the Overlook. The sense that suddenly something might just appear before you; a horrific image that might just send you out of your mind.

But the only ghosts were the ones I brought with me.

As is the case for everyone.

Room 305.

Inside, the big bastard raised his head to look

176

at us. His face was bloodied. His nose was pulped and cauliflowered across his face. Can't say it made him any more or less ugly. The fact that he wasn't wearing any clothes didn't help matters.

He looked at me as I walked in. His lips parted. He might have snarled. He knew who I was.

I didn't look at him. Not directly.

He had been my price. My negotiating tool. The cops who raided the house would say he was the one who got away. But they had no idea where he was. They thought I just wanted to talk to him. They didn't know that the old man was involved. That the bruiser might not see the morning.

Malone was leaning on the cricket bat in the same way that Patrick MacNee would lean on his umbrella during the glory days of *The Avengers*. He smiled as we entered the room. 'A good workout,' he said. 'Nothing like it.'

Burns said nothing. He crouched before the naked man and looked into his eyes. The two men stared at each other. The big bastard was defiant. He was in pain, but remained resolute in his silence.

Burns said, 'You know who I am?'

The man spat. His phlegm was red.

Burns smiled.

I stood near the door. Watched. Remained impassive as I could.

'No one can hear us,' Burns said.

'I think he's worked that one out,' Malone said. Smug. He stepped away. Bowed his head towards Burns. An invitation.

The old man rarely got his hands dirty. Only in the most extreme of situations. Like the year before when he personally took it upon himself to murder a child killer. His morals so offended that he didn't want anyone else to have the pleasure. Some things you have to do yourself.

Burns got in close to the other man. 'Whatever you tell me, it remains here. Between us. No one will know you talked. And if they do find out, no one will blame you. My friend here, the cricketer, he can be . . . persuasive.'

'He's a fucking pussy.' Spitting out the words. Real effort to talk.

Burns said, 'Would you like some water?'

'Fuck . . . you.'

'A little food? I can send one of my pals here for a pizza. Or a kebab. You look like a kebab man. A few pints and a doner? Can't blame you.'

Silence.

Burns said, 'Oh, I can't touch you, can I? You're a hard man.' He stood up. 'Oh, yes, Mr White. You're a hard man. I know all about you. About your wife. Divorced, of course. She didn't like the idea of you doing what you do. She thought you were a security guard. A night watchman. That all you did was hang around empty building sites – much like this one – and maybe listen to some music. Read magazines. She wouldn't even have minded if they were dirty magazines. After all, books require too much thought, don't they? And you're not big on thinking. I know why she divorced you. I know the reasons on the papers and the reasons that no one ever fucking talked

178

about. Especially you. Because you think she exaggerated the truth. Maybe I should ask her one day. You wouldn't mind me talking to her? Or maybe one of my associates?' He talked calmly. Conversationally. The words tripped lightly from his lips. This was how he got before the real violence began. The snake ceasing its rattling.

I wondered when he had the time to learn about this man's life.

There were resources he had that amazed me. He understood the power not just of physical strength, but of knowledge.

White continued his defiant stare, although he knew better than to try and stand. In this place, he was without power. All he could was stay down and stay quiet. Hope the end came quick.

I had promised Susan that no one would die.

Had she known I was lying?

Had I?

Burns said, 'Maybe that doesn't upset you. And maybe she wouldn't tell me the truth, anyway. There must be someone else we could talk to? Maybe . . . your daughter?'

That did it. White roared and clambered to his feet. Halfway up when Malone swung that bat, caught the big bastard in the stomach. White roared, doubled and collapsed again.

Burns said, 'Are you ready to talk now, Mr White? We don't have to talk about you at all. Just a friend of yours. Craig Nairn. Tell me where he is, no one will hurt you again. I promise. And no one will need to talk to your daughter. How old is she now? Thirteen? How long since you last saw her?'

The big bastard's head dipped. For a moment, I could see his eyes and see the defiance fade. Every man has a weak spot. And it's not always physical. Watch enough movies, you start to think that every conflict can be resolved by fisticuffs. But most men are stopped by their emotions. Even the ones they refuse to talk about.

Burns hunkered down again. He said, 'Just an address. That's all.'

White talked.

When he was done, Burns nodded. He stood up. 'I said no one would ever hurt you again. That's almost true.' He nodded at Malone. Malone grabbed the defeated man's head and pulled it back. In his free hand, he had a knife. He plunged the blade through the man's eye and into his brain. The man struggled for a moment and then went limp.

The smell of shit and piss filled the room. Tickled at the nostrils, made you want to vomit. I tried not to react but my legs started to give way. I swallowed a sour taste.

As we left the room, Burns put his arm around me. 'If they want to ignore the rules then we have to do the same. Except we have to be even worse than they are. You don't win a gunfight armed with a fucking cricket bat. They think I'm a tired old fucker resting on his reputation. They're going to learn the fucking truth.'

Thirty-Six

The old high rises were coming down. Once dominant on Dundee's skyline on approach from the West, the old symbols of poverty and hopelessness – in the twenty-first century, it was hard to believe they were conceived as part of a shiny, utopian future – were being demolished. One by one, they were disappearing. Old mistakes being erased in the hope that no one would remember them. In their place, the council had created shiny little villages and called them estates. With the blue plastic window frames and the clean brickwork, these new council houses felt cleaner and safer than the old high rises with their rickety lifts and corridors daubed with graffiti. But it was tempting to wonder whether all anyone had done was brush the old problems under the carpet, and apply a fresh coat of paint. Sooner or later, the old issues would come back to the surface. But for now these new estates seemed hopeful, busy and thriving.

The address that White gave us was a low-roofed bungalow along a street of similar looking houses. A small driveway, but no sign of a car. A trampoline dominated the front garden, such as it was. The woman who lived at the address had two kids. Rumours said the children were Nairn's, but she had always claimed the father to be another man who had vanished some 8 years earlier, after the birth of the second child. A waster. A drug addict. A man who was bound to disappear sooner or later. Probably not through his own volition.

I walked to the front door myself. The old man waited further down the street with Malone. Out of sight.

I tapped out six short raps. Stepped back. Resisted the urge to pull out ID, like I was still on the force.

The woman who answered wore hooped earrings and a fake tan that was beginning to streak just a little. Her naturally dark hair showed at the roots, contrasting with the bottle blonde curls that were sprayed to within an inch of their lives and hooked stiffly around her shoulders.

'Aye?'

'I'm looking for Craig Nairn.'

'Nut,' she said. 'Don't ken that name.' Bad liar. She did, of course. Her eyes gave it away. She was terrified. Of me? I was sure she wasn't scared of Nairn.

'I'm not police.'

'Don't care. No one here called Craig, right? So fuck off. Sharp-like.'

I shrugged. Shouted past her, 'Tell him it's McNee.'

Nairn came down from upstairs. Slow. Cautious. His head forward so he could get a good look and see it really was me. 'The fuck d'you want? The fuck did you find me here?'

'Jesus, Craig, someone's going to see—'

'Shut up, and go watch telly. Me and this man need to have a wee chat.' He was smiling. Maybe still convinced of his own hard man image. Thinking he'd fooled me the other night.

The woman looked ready to argue but then just shook her head and walked away. Her bare feet didn't make a sound on the laminated wood flooring.

Nairn said, 'You really are a detective. How the fuck'd'you work out I was here? Or did we rattle your brain pan so hard you actually got smart?' Cocky. Arrogant. Believing his own press.

'A wee birdie told me.'

'Aye?'

'Oh, aye.' That wasn't me. Another voice from behind me. Low baritone. Cracked with age but still conveying the strength and brutality on which its owner had made its name.

Nairn made to bolt.

I lunged in, grabbed at his legs, tripped him on the stairs. Poor man's rugby tackle. But it worked. He landed hard.

'What the fu—' The bottle blonde came back out to have a go at me and her man, stopped talking when she saw Burns and Malone.

Malone said, 'You and me, darling, are going to go check on the kiddies, aye? While these lads have a little chat.' He stepped towards her. She backed off.

On the stairs, Nairn made a moaning sound. Sounding like a child who's been caught hiding the remains of his mother's good china under the bed after weeks of protesting his innocence as to where it had gone.

Thirty-Seven

The bedroom upstairs. Curtains drawn. Nairn on a seat in a corner. He already knew he was dead. His eyes were red. His cheeks wet.

He said, 'So what now?' Still shooting for defiance. Still missing.

'Now what happens is that you tell me how a little bumshite like you managed to become some kind of black market genius.' The old man no longer taking the softly-softly approach. Not with this one.

Nairn hesitated.

The old man kept his distance. 'Forget the girls. Forget the details. None of what you claim to control is within your power. You're a front, son. A friendly, local face. Right? Those girls, the ones we're going to forget, you wouldn't have the nous to get them inside the border never mind set them up in a wee pad like that. You were never smart, son. I remember how you used to come round begging for work. How you'd do anything to get in with me and mine.'

'And you turned me away.' A flash of anger there. A spark of defiance. But short-lived and half-hearted.

'Aye, and can you blame me? You've been in and out of the wee lad's courts all your life. Petty fucking shite every time. You're pond scum, Craig Nairn. You think you're a fucking shark and the truth is you're nothing more than a goldfish arsing around in its bowl. Forgetting every three seconds just how limited its life really is.'

Nairn didn't say anything.

'You're not working alone, lad. Tell me who's backing you. Maybe I can find it in my heart to show some mercy. You know, for the sake of the wee kids downstairs.'

'Go fuck yourself.'

'Tell me, son. This is your last chance. You get that, aye? You're not so dense that you can't?'

'And what, you'll let me live?'

'We'll see.'

'I know about you,' Nairn said. Fighting back tears. Cheeks scarlet. Every breath was an effort as he tried not to burst into tears.

It had been too easy to find Nairn. His attack on Mary Burns had been blunt and obvious. Not in keeping with the strategy that had been used to attack the old man's empire.

We could kill Nairn. But it wouldn't make a difference. I could see that, now. Before the old man even thought about ending Nairn's life, he needed to know who the real enemy was.

'I know about you,' Nairn said, again. 'You're a fucking monster. A liar. You always lie. You kill people because they're no longer useful to you. You're just like the Zombie. Just fucking like him.'

'Say that again.'

'Fuck you.'

'The Zombie?'

'Fuck you, old man. Your time is past. You

185

know that, aye? You're not the biggest and baddest fucker around anymore.'

'That so?'

'Oh, aye.'

Burns turned to look at me. 'You know who the Zombie is, right?' He looked ready to laugh. Same as if Nairn had said he was working for Dracula or Lucifer.

I knew the name. Of course I knew. The Zombie was an underworld bogeyman. A myth. A constant reference in police files across the country, but never seen or caught. He had been implicated in some of the biggest international conspiracies that the authorities had ever known. His name was attached to drug cartels and weapons deals and people-trafficking. He was linked to trade in organs, and murder for hire. But every time the authorities heard his name, he was nowhere to be found.

Like T.S. Elliot's Macavity the Mystery Cat, every time they turned around, the Zombie wasn't there.

Thirty-Eight

Zsomobor Bako

The Zombie.

One of Hungary's most vicious gangsters, he had cut a path of blood and misery across eastern Europe. The eldest son of a poor family living in one of Budapest's most deprived areas, he made his name as a killer by the time he turned twenty. Killed without emotion and without hesitation. They called him the Zombie because nothing affected him. When one of his victims' families killed his parents in retaliation, Bako approached one of the most senior men in the Hungarian mafia and asked for permission to kill the family in revenge. The senior gangster asked Bako if he was looking for revenge for himself. Bako said that it was not about revenge. It was about showing that he could not be touched. There would be consequences for anyone who crossed him.

Within two years the senior gangster was dead by Bako's hand. He had failed to learn the lessons of that first meeting. Had treated the Zombie like he would any other psychopath for hire. Failed to see the man's ambition.

International effort across Europe appeared to do little to dent Bako's organizations. He dealt in drugs, people, weapons, organs, whatever his clients could afford to pay for. Cross his palm with currency and anything was possible. When one of his many ventures was halted, another sprung up in its place. Through fear, intimidation and outright brutality, the Zombie absorbed others' criminal enterprises, made them his own.

The man disappeared into modern legend. Like a wraith. A shadow. A ghost. At first the authorities had thought he was just another would-be kingpin who would disappear like the rest; a victim of his own overstretched ambition and greed. But the dead-eye certainty with which he had built his reputation served Bako well. He resisted the temptations and ego-fuelled mistakes that others might have made. He built his empire slowly. Carefully. Brutally.

The more power he gained, the more invisible he became. The police would often come close to finding him, only to have him vanish at the last second. Always leaving some little sign of his presence. Enough to taunt the authorities. Like the Cheshire cat's smile, but the teeth were bloodied and rotten instead of gleaming and white.

In recent years, some of Bako's organizations had tried to infiltrate Scotland the same way they had managed to gain a foothold in London and the South of England. Most of these efforts had been unsuccessful. But Bako was not one for backing down.

And now he was gunning for the old man.

Thirty-Nine

'You're not lying to me, are you?'

'Whatever you do, you old fart, it's nothing compared to what he would do to me if I rolled over.'

'Oh you'll roll over, you prick. Like a good wee dog. Tell me, whose idea was the fucking bomb?'

Nairn shrugged. 'Everything would have been fine if you hadn't started this. If you'd left me alone, there would have been enough for everyone.'

That wasn't the way Bako worked, of course. The psycho wouldn't share the land with anyone.

Then again, neither would Burns. Not unless it suited him to do so. I still remembered the turf wars he'd engaged in while establishing his own operations. The long list of names of those who had opposed him.

It was just that he used a surgical knife where men like Bako used dynamite.

'It was the bogeyman's idea,' Burns said. 'Wasn't it? You wouldn't know an original thought if it kicked you in the bloody balls.'

Nairn said nothing.

'How do you and Bako communicate?'

Nothing.

'What kind of a cut do you get?'

Nothing.

'Oh, you're a hard man, now? Fine. That's fine. You won't talk to me, it doesn't matter. But you'll talk to my friend.'

Nairn laughed. Looked at me. 'Him? Little goody two shoes? All he can do is watch and keep his mouth shut. He's not like you, old man. Fucking hell, he's not even like me. Had to call for help rather than take care of business himself.' He cocked his head to one side. 'Who were they, anyway? They weren't with this old fart.'

I said nothing.

Burns left the room.

Did the old man expect me to do something? To prove his faith in me?

Nairn and I regarded each other. Lions sizing up the opponent.

I said, 'I read your file. I used to be police. I

still have friends. Want to know something, Nairn? You were a nobody. Now you're acting like king shite. Even if you do have a little help from the Zombie. And I know you think that Burns will kill you anyway. That whatever he does, it won't be worse than what Bako has in store for anyone who betrays him. You're in over your head. And you're scared shitless. I mean, you're putting up a front, but it's there. In your eyes.'

'You have a point?' He hesitated just a little. Maybe I was getting to him. Pop psychology paying off.

'Aye, I do. You think you have only two options. I'm your third.'

'You?'

'Like I said, I still have connections. I can ensure your safety.'

'Those cunts turned up at the old fart's place?'

I smiled. 'What do you think?'

'Police,' he said. 'I fucking knew it. You're a strange prick of a man, McNee.'

Was that a compliment? His voice sounded warm with admiration.

'So what do you want?'

'You tell me what he wants to know. I tell him I'll take care of you. And you disappear.'

'Aye?'

'Bus. Train. Whatever. You get the fuck out of here and don't come back. No one ever looks for you because everyone thinks you're dead. Buried somewhere out in Templeton Woods, maybe. Or face down at the bottom of the Tay, pockets filled with rocks and eyes bulging out of your skull.'

'And what's to stop me from telling the old man what you've done? What's to stop me telling him that you're a traitor?' He sounded eager. Brain cells firing. Thinking he had an advantage.

I leaned forward. 'He'll kill us both. We both know how strong your sense of self-preservation is. And I might just kill you my fucking self if you try.'

He thought about this for a moment. I let him stew.

What would Burns be expecting to find on his return? That I had beaten this poor prick to a bloody pulp? That I had threatened his family? His friends?

Was this a test? What happened if I failed?

The old man was in the middle of a war he had never wanted to fight. His defences were up. His enemies had committed the ultimate atrocity. All bets were off.

What did he expect of his soldiers? What did he expect of me?

The door opened.

Quicker than I thought. Had he been listening for the sounds of screams?

Burns and Malone walked in. The old man smiled. Showing off his incisors. Said, 'Oh, I wasn't talking about this one.' He nodded at me to get out. Then turned to Malone. 'This here is the man who will get you talking. I don't think anyone's ever not told him what he wants to hear.'

'You lying fuck!' Nairn yelled. At me. 'You fuck! You promised me! You promised—'

The rest of his words were muffled as Burns shut the door behind us. 'Come on, son,' he said. 'Let's go have a wee coffee. Have a little fun with the bairns. Forget about this wee cunt for a while.'

We walked down the stairs. The noises from behind the closed door made me want to run.

Forty

The kids buzzed toys around the floor, occasionally lifting them and waving them around as though desperate to share the joy. The old man hunkered down with them for a while. He pushed the toys around, imitated the noises they made and laughed with them. The kids took to him as though he were a favourite uncle who came around every day.

I was a more uncertain presence. They stared up at me with wide eyes as though I was a giant come down from the beanstalk with the express intention of grinding their bones to make my bread. I tried my best to smile with them, but I didn't understand the toys, and the sheer uncomplicated joy they expressed made me feel sad. A nostalgic emptiness. For lost innocence I could no longer remember.

Their mother – her name was Chantelle – sat on the edge of the sofa. She didn't take her eyes off the boys once. Her body language was tense: posture stiff and unyielding. She wanted me and the old man out of the house, but was too afraid to speak up. And the old man's apparent pleasure in playing with her children was even more unsettling.

We all knew what was happening upstairs. But what could any of us really do about it? Burns was the man in control. We followed his lead.

The sounds that came from upstairs were muffled, but unsettling. The kids didn't seem to notice, but Chantelle and I jumped in our seats at every thump and moan. There were some sounds that might have been screams, but they kept cutting off with a sense of finality that made us wonder whether it was finally over.

The old man didn't react. He laughed and joked and stole the kid's noses.

Finally, we heard footsteps. Malone was drying off his hands with a towel when he came through the door. 'It's done,' he said. Like he'd just repaired the boiler.

Burns stood up. Ruffled the hair on the two wee boy's heads. Said, 'They'll be taken care of, lass. Don't you worry about that.'

Chantelle looked at him, eyes wide, stuck between shock and hatred. She let us leave without saying another word.

In the car, we were silent. I was in the back seat. Kept my eye on Malone the whole journey, worried about what he might say.

What had Nairn told him?

I'd taken a risk talking to Nairn the way I had. But I meant what I said. He was a nasty wee prick, but he'd been in over his head. One way or the other, he had to disappear. I wasn't about to have a third man's death on my conscience.

I had thought I could save Nairn. From Burns, if not from himself. But I must have known what would happen. Looking back, I saw the inevitability of it all. Nairn was a footnote. He was a pawn. A small player in a far larger game. From the word go, he'd been destined to end his life

Burns called for a clean-up crew before we left the house. After he'd done that, he gently told Chantelle what would happen if she talked to the police. She understood, of course. Given who her boyfriend had been, she was well aware that talking to the coppers was the equivalent of sticking a gun in your mouth and pulling the trigger.

Kind of like offering mercy to a man that David Burns wanted dead.

We drove through the city. Parked at the rear of the city-centre office block that housed Burns Enterprises. Walked to the third floor. In the lift, I stood between the two other men. Trapped. No way I could get out of this one.

To get to Burns's private office you walked through an open plan workspace that was busy during the day with office drones on phones and computer screens. Officially Burns ran a construction business. How he'd managed to get so deeply involved in the city's rejuvenation plans. How he became so integral to the lifeblood of Dundee. He pumped money and funds to those who needed it. In public he spoke of his pride at being from the city. He attended games at Dens Park. Donated part of his legal profits to the club. Acted like he meant every word. 'Dundonian through and through,' he once said, when asked to describe himself. 'And proud of it.'

No wonder the police hated him. He was a symbol of civic pride at the same time as being a drug dealer and a known criminal. The disparity between those public images should have been impossible to maintain, and yet he managed it with apparent effortlessness. He was every copper's worst nightmare: a criminal beloved by the people.

The old man made sure the office door was locked before he sat behind the desk. Malone moved smoothly, as though he knew what he was doing. Unlocked a battered old cabinet unit, pulled down the rolltop and poured three glasses of whiskey from a crystal decanter. Took one straight to the old man, indicated I should help myself to one of the others remaining.

I did so.

We drank in silence. And quickly.

Burns said, 'Bako.' He shook his head. His eyes were focussed somewhere on the middle distance. He didn't care if we were listening. He needed to work this through in his own mind. 'Jesus fucking Christ. Say what you like about me – and people have – but I've got rules. This new breed of arsehole doesn't give a fuck. Get off on the pain they cause.'

I'd heard people say similar things about Burns. But maybe it's also true that old age mellows a man.

Burns said to Malone, 'What did Nairn tell you?'

195

'That this prick tried to offer him a deal.' Nodding in my direction.

This was it, then. No way out. Like Nairn, looked like my life had only ever been leading in one direction. And this was it.

The old man laughed. 'A deal?'

'Said that our pal here would let him live if he gave everything up. All Nairn had to do was pretend he'd been knocked around.'

'Priceless,' Burns said. Then he looked at me, expression stony. 'You still think you're one of the good guys, don't you? Maybe you are. I know enough cops on the job would have hurt a man like Nairn without thinking twice. But even without the constraints of your own rules, you still look for an alternative. It's touching. Stupid, aye. But touching.'

Jesus, it didn't even cross his mind that the deal I offered Nairn might have been serious.

What did that say about how he saw me?

Malone said, 'He also said that he never met Bako face to face. Only talked to the bastard through representatives. First time, it was three Ukranian fucks. Offered him a choice. He could do what Bako asked, or be an example to the next man.'

'Maybe our wee friend wasn't so stupid after all,' said Burns.

I said nothing. Just listened. The invisible man in the room. There by virtue of being in the right place at the right time. I wasn't part of the old man's war council. What I had to say was of no real interest. I did not truly understand such matters. But I was worth keeping close. Long as my mouth remained shut.

196

The Ukranians gave Nairn a number. It changed every few days. The number arrived by text to Nairn's phone whenever it was updated. It did not connect directly to Bako, but to one of his operatives. The man behind the man.

The number was due to change again in twenty-four hours.

It was the best route to Bako.

'This is going to get worse before it gets better,' the old man said. 'I know I value my isolation these days. But you can't hide away all your life like the bloody Elephant Man. Pretend you don't exist. Sooner or later you have to come out into the sunshine. Let your enemies know, this is who I am.' He smiled. 'We're going to expose this fucker. Hang him out the way they used to. Stick his bastard head on a fucking pike at the border and say, "No more!" Oh, aye, what those English pricks did to Willie Wallace will look like a fucking brush with Ken Dodd's tickle stick.' He looked at me as though realizing for the first time that I was in the room. 'This isn't for you, son. You proved that with Nairn. So I want you to go back to your wee police safe house. Wherever it is. Where you left my wife. I know you trust the people you left her with, but the fact is I don't fucking know them.' He stood up, walked over and placed a hand on my shoulder. Direct eye contact. 'I'm not palming you off, son. I know you think its shite. That I don't trust you. But you're not the man for the work ahead. You protect people. That's who you are. You do what-ever you need to do that. You don't have the motivation to go up against this Hungarian shiteball. So I'm asking you to do what you do best. Look out for the innocent. For my wife.'

Was it a crock of shit? Hard to tell with a man whose own internal motivations were constantly up for re-evaluation.

I couldn't argue with him, though. There were things you could fake in the name of an assignment, and others that you couldn't. Going against your personality, your own set of ethical and moral motivations was almost impossible. The best undercover officers had something of the criminal inside them already. They could allow themselves to betray standard ethical and moral behaviours in order to achieve their goals.

I couldn't do that. There were lines I could not cross.

Lines that men like David Burns couldn't even see.

Forty-One

I gave the knock. Waited. They would identify me from the security footage. The man who answered the safe house door was young. Too young for me to remember him from the bad old days on the force. But he knew who I was. Guess I'd become station lore. A cautionary tale for hotheaded young uniforms. He insisted on patting me down in the front hall before allowing me further access. Taking no chances.

In the kitchen, two more plainclothes stared at each other over cards. Betting on pound coins. They probably wanted a beer or two, the chance to make some jokes, turn this dull assignment into something more memorable.

I found Mary in the back room watching television. A mid-afternoon chat show. The presenter was safely camp; utterly inoffensive. The kind of man who wouldn't threaten or challenge you. Except perhaps with a cheeky double entendre or two where he could get away with it.

Mary looked up as I came in.

'She's not here.'

I didn't understand.

'The girl. Susan.'

'I'm here to talk to you.'

'Oh.'

I sat down next to her. The presenter read out reader's letters. Showed off some of the daft things that people sent him including a knitted doll that was supposed to be a good likeness. Even I had to laugh at the lack of skill. But the audience's laughter was gentle, perhaps because they all knew that their efforts would be just as bad. If not worse.

'You're not here,' Mary said.

'No,' I said. 'Just thinking.'

'About anything except her?'

'What are you? An agony aunt?'

'No. But I am a middle-aged woman whose husband is hardly in the house any more. It gives me pleasure to interfere in other people's lives.' Maybe she wanted to smile, but she suppressed it. Except around the eyes.

'You know the truth about me?'

'That you're spying?' She lost the hint of the smile. 'Same as Ernie was? I know. My husband suspects it. But you're just like Ernie, son. Heartbreaking, in its way. You're a compassionate man. You want to see David for a criminal but can't help seeing the whole man.'

'He's still done bad things.'

'And maybe you'll take him down. But what I mean is that we know what you're here to do. It's your job. But for him, it's a game of chess, I think.'

I shook my head. Feeling foolish.

'I don't say anything to him. He doesn't say anything to me. Maybe that's why it works for us; the fact that we don't talk about his other business. He knows I know. I know he knows. That's enough. The same way that some couples have hobbies and interests the other one doesn't understand.'

'You have your painting, he has his kneecapping?'

She laughed. The first time I'd heard her laugh. It was gentle. A light piano riff. 'You're making fun of us.'

'That obvious?'

'Tell me this: if he didn't do things that you disagreed with, would you like him?'

I thought about it for a while. The old man could be genuinely charming. There was a reason that the legitimate side of his interests had done so well. He was a man who made connections. He had the ability to make people genuinely like him. He could be ruthless, but then so could many

200

otherwise legit people. He had a temper. I could relate to that. But one on one, he was charming. Had a spark in his eye that made you think of your grandfather. Seeing him with Nairn's children had been an odd contrast to the way that he dealt with their father. Like he was two different people in one body.

'Yes,' I said. 'In a way.'

'Then you understand.'

'No.'

She patted my knee. 'You're still young.'

We looked at the television again.

She said, 'You avoided my question.'

'I think I answered it.'

'No, about her.'

Meaning Susan. The question she had asked should been simple to answer. But I couldn't think of a simple thing to say.

'It doesn't do any good,' I said, 'running over the past.'

'Because you're scared of how you'll look?'

'Maybe. Look, things between me and her got complicated.'

'And yet she came running when you asked.'

'Like I said: complicated.'

Mary laughed. 'I don't know if it's me or the world, but I can't remember when love became complicated. Back when I was your age, what we did was admit we liked each other and then work through everything else.'

'Just like that?'

'Just like that.'

I shook my head. It couldn't have been that simple for her. Not with a man like Burns. But then maybe me and Susan just needed to get over ourselves. Maybe Mary had a point.

I stood up. 'You want coffee?'

'Tea for me. Milk. Two sugars.'

I went to the kitchen. The young lad was in there leaning on the counter, checking his mobile. I said, 'Signal's bad out here.'

'Wi-fi.'

'Right.'

I hit the kettle.

There was a knock at the door. 'Expecting someone?'

He shook his head. 'Nah. But we get it every so often from the old duffer next door. Wanting to borrow salt or something. Bollocks every time. Reckon he's just lonely. Doesn't get out much. Hasn't really twigged that it's never the same person answers the door.' He sighed. 'I'll just tell him to piss off, eh?'

'Or you could give him the salt.'

He looked at me like I was crazy. 'Know who pays for the salt in this place? We have to account for every fucking grain.'

He left the room. I busied myself with the kettle. Pulled open cupboards searching for the sugar. They could charge me if they liked.

I heard the front door open. Waited for the mumble of conversation.

Dropped the sugar as the bullets flew. High velocity. Deep thrumming noise as they shattered the air out in the confined corridor.

I dropped.

There were yells. Screams.

Automatic weapons.

A year earlier, I had been at the heart of a hostage situation when an armed response unit burst through the door. The noise had had a brutal physicality that rattled through my bones.

This sounded worse. More violent. More random. More deadly. The Armed Response coppers had been careful about picking their targets. They'd been well trained. Organized. This bunch sounded trigger happy.

There were two exits from the kitchen. The second would take me around to the rear of the living room. The men with the guns would be heading straight for the front door if they took the main hall. I could cut round the back way, get to Mary before they did.

I kept low, crouched as I pushed through the door, made for cover behind the sofa. Mary was on the floor, hands over her head. She looked at me with wide eyes. I gestured for her to come with me. She didn't move. I could see the tension threatening to burst out of her. She wanted to scream, but her self-preservation was too strong. Any noise would only bring the predators into the room.

I snapped. 'Come on!'

The words got through to her. She scrabbled towards me. I held out my hand. She took it. We went out low towards the rear entrance.

Straight into a pair of dark jeans. Slowly, I stood up. Grabbed Mary's hand, brought her up with me. The thug's hair was thinning, forced down flat with what could have been chip-grease. He smiled. He was holding a rifle in his hands. The muzzle pointed down. No need for posture.

His eyes told me everything I needed to know. He said, 'The police are dead. You cannot run.' Hint of a European accent. Hungarian? I couldn't really tell. But his English was good. Probably naturalized. He had to be working for Bako. Explained the gear. The violence. The accent. The fact that Burns wouldn't send someone to kill his own wife.

Would he?

It had always been a hypothetical question between me and Ernie after a few pints down the Phoenix: what would the old man do if his wife turned traitor? The old man had always given this big talk about how important family was and loyalty. Yet we knew he would happily kill anyone who dared cross him. Without compassion. Without exception.

So what about his wife? What would happen to her? Would he send the boys round?

It wasn't outside the realms of possibility. For all his talk.

Maybe he did have some kind of condition. Or maybe he was just more in touch with his own violence than the rest of us. Or maybe he was just plain bad. The kind of evil fuck we all read about in the reports, the witness testimony. Maybe it was the violence that was the real Burns, where all the talk of loyalty, graft and family was the posturing.

So I had to hope these guys were working for Bako.

For Mary's sake.

Forty-Two

They bundled us into the back of a car. Blindfolded. Directed by rough hands.

I wondered if we would look suspicious to other drivers. Would anyone notice that something was wrong? I hadn't seen the car they threw us into. Maybe the windows were tinted. No one seemed to stop us along the way. Not noticing or not caring. We rolled along at what seemed like a normal pace. No sharp turns. No sudden or unexpected bursts of speed.

If I was a movie hero, a John McClane type, I might have made some dumb-ass move, try overpowering the guys with the guns. Maybe wound up rolling out a moving vehicle, holding Mary close to protect her at the car slammed into a wall at speed and burst into an improbably fireball.

All of this, of course while blindfolded. And, if I really was John McClane, shoeless as well.

But I was just an ordinary man in his late thirties. I'd taken my share of violence. And dished some out as well. The truth was, I made a move any of these bastards didn't like, I'd end up dead. Either with a bullet or just with my neck snapped or throat sliced. The only moves I could make were to keep still and keep cooperative.

The drive took about twenty-five minutes. We were pulled out of the car and on to uneven ground.

Forced to walk by men who pushed us around roughly. I nearly went down twice, my feet failing to gain purchase on broken paving slabs.

We were led into a place with bare floors. The rough hands forced us upstairs. I figured the building for residential in design, but currently unoccupied. I didn't know where we were. Were we still within the city limits?

Finally we were shoved into a room that had been carpeted. Recently. I could see a little beneath the bottom of the blindfold. The carpet had that quality of being freshly laid. No stains, the fibres still strong.

Our blindfolds were ripped off. I blinked a few times. Brought the world back into focus. Got my bearings as best I could. Mary was next to me. Trying to remain stoic. She may have claimed that her greatest fear was that her husband would come home in a body bag; now she was every bit as frightened for her own life.

Did she know who Bako was? Did she know his reputation?

The room was laid out like an office. Big desk. Carpeted floors. Walls hung with prints of city scenes from around the globe. A laptop on the desk humming quietly away. Even a plant. They'd turned a shell of a building into a home away from home with all the unique personality of a Travel Lodge reception.

Behind the desk, a man sat bolt upright in a leather chair. His hands were on the desk, palms down. He had a peculiar expression as he looked at me and Mary Burns: a scientist scrutinizing the subjects of his latest experiment.

He was thin. His face was gaunt; a young Christopher Lee. His eyes were sunk back in his head, giving him a corpse-like appearance. I remembered an undertaker telling me once how after death, the eyes dipped deeper into the skull. How you had to force them up again for funerals to give the illusion of life.

This, then, was the Zombie.

Sharp suit, tie tight round his neck, shirt and jacket fitted impeccably. I imagined he had a row of identical suits all pressed and steamed and ready to go each morning. He probably changed clothes at least three times a day to ensure he always gave off the perfect impression. I'd met men like him before. Most of them in finance.

You finally meet the bogeyman and he looks like the manager of your local bank.

No one had ever seen Bako. As he disappeared into his own legend, so any traces he had left behind vanished as well. All anyone had ever seen were old, blurred photos. They could have been the man in front of me. But maybe not. All the same, this man spoke with the authority of the Zombie. And maybe my doubts came from my recent dealings with Nairn. When people lie to you enough times, you find it hard to believe that anyone is telling the truth.

Bako said, 'You will not be harmed.' Heavily accented. But his syntax and grammar were impeccable.

'That's reassuring.'

'I was talking to Mrs Burns.'

I shut my mouth. But it was too late. He smiled.

He'd got to me. My first mistake. Certainly wasn't going to be my last.

'You will not be harmed,' he said again, ignoring me. 'All your husband has to do is agree to work with us. That is all. We will share his operations, his income. He will have a good life. If he does what he is told.'

Mary said nothing.

Bako turned to look at me. Grinned. His teeth were dental-work white. 'And you, my friend . . . I know who you are. What you are. You have been working against Burns, have you not? You are a police informant. He has been a fool not to kill you. Maybe he has sentimental feelings?'

I hoped to God that Bako was as much of a fool as the old man.

'But you are a man whose morality is flexible. I know you, Mr McNee. Have heard about you. You have killed. Broken the laws you once upheld. Perhaps there is hope for you. A place for you.'

He was messing with me. Say yes, and I was a traitor to my old boss. Say no and he would kill me.

As I weighed my options, the door opened. A woman entered. Tall, elegant, long, dark hair brushed straight down her back. In her mid-forties, maybe, but looking good on it. She wore little makeup but her skin was flawless. She walked to Bako, leaned down and whispered something in his ear. He nodded, and then dismissed her with a wave of his hand.

She looked at me as she walked out the room.

208

Her eyes were cold. I thought of lizards, of a snake regarding a small animal as a potential snack.

Bako gestured to one of the three men who had brought us here. The man leaned close while Bako said something that I didn't understand. The big man laughed.

He walked up to me and said, 'Come.'

'Where?'

'To pub. For drink.'

Everyone in the room laughed. Except Mary. And me.

Forty-Three

They threw me into an empty room. No furniture. Windows blocked out by dark material that had been stapled roughly to the frame.

They locked the door. Left me alone.

Old psychological trick. Gets you imagining worse might actually be coming. Softens you up for the main feature.

I took a deep breath. Still no idea where I was. I got to my feet. As I did so, my chest tightened. I took a deep breath. The sensation eased. I moved over to the window, prised my fingers beneath the cloth and pulled it back gently so I could see what was outside.

I got grey sky. A few branches. No sense of what floor I was on, how far it was to the ground.

And then the door opened. I let go of the

material and it snapped back into place, eliminating that one sliver of the outside world.

'Mr McNee.' Bako. Flanked by the same thug who'd thrown me in here. 'You are an interesting man.'

'I'd normally take that as a compliment.'

'It is not.'

Bako closed the door. His thug stood quietly in the corner. Clasped his hands in front of his stomach. Did a great impression of a statue. He was built like Desperate Dan. Give him a red shirt and cowboy hat, he'd have a great chance with a second career entertaining at children's parties.

'You are flexible. Morally speaking.'

'Aye?'

'You were police. Then you went into business for yourself. Still serving the law. You had principles. You put away some very bad men. Some very bad policemen, too.'

So he knew who I was. It wasn't like I was a state secret. Some of my cases had made the papers. He wouldn't have to dig too deep to get that kind of information. So far, so unimpressive.

'And?'

'And then you work for Mr Burns. This seems to me an odd choice. Yes?'

'Your English is excellent, Mr Bako.'

'So is my French. My German. My Russian.'

'A polyglot.'

'Big word for such a man.'

'Aye?'

'A man of violence.'

'You're confusing me with yourself.'

'Perhaps. But my violence is necessary. When you deal with the basest of human instincts, you must adapt to your environment. Your violence is personal. The man you shot, for example. He threatened your life. The lives of those you were close to.'

'I can't say it wasn't satisfying. But I had no choice.'

'And the corrupt policeman?'

'That wasn't me. I don't know who killed him.' Although I had my suspicions. Susan was the last person to be seen with former Deputy Chief Constable Wood. She had wanted to kill him after realizing he was directly responsible for the death of her father. But I never knew if she carried through on that need. All I knew was that someone roasted the poor bastard alive. And given the revelations that came about after his death, no one had been in a position to mourn his death, never mind search too hard for a killer.

'Really? You have no idea?'

'Really.'

Bako nodded. 'I offer you a choice.'

'The same choice you offered Craig Nairn?'

'You're a much smarter man. Yes, the same choice. This city, you know it. The people, the customs, the appetites. You have seen both its civilized surface and the underbelly of vice. You are perfectly placed to work for me.'

'And, as you already said, I'm morally adaptable?'

He smiled. All teeth. Perfectly aligned teeth.

I said, 'There were rumours that you had died. That your empire just continued without you.'

'Print the legend. Is that not what they say?'

'Sure,' I said. 'What's wrong with theatricality?'

That grin again.

The door opened. The woman walked in. She had an assured presence. More even than Bako. The way she moved made my spine shiver. She looked at me. Then Bako. Whispered in the man's ear.

I wouldn't have understood, even if I could hear.

Bako looked at me. Then he looked at the thug. Gave the other man a small nod. Barely more than a flick of the head.

The thug nodded. Impassive.

Bako and the woman left the room.

The thug stepped forward.

I braced myself. Clenched my fists. But I was already defeated. My story would end here, in an empty room. Alone, with no one to know or care. Just me and a man who saw me as a piece of meat to be bloodied and broken.

Did I deserve any better?

This was about making an example of me. Others would know that I died in pain and alone in an empty room. I would become part of the Bako legend.

I would be the unknown soldier of the war between two powerful, utterly amoral men.

The thug grinned. His teeth were yellow. Incisors sharp. He said something I didn't understand.

I braced myself.

Just one or two good punches. Draw some

blood. Blacken an eye. I would be happy with that.

He reached into his pocket, pulled a butterfly knife. 'I am artist,' he said, in English. 'Body is canvas.'

I swallowed. Focussed only on the knife. The blade.

The thug feinted a swing. I flinched. He laughed. The knife cut only air. 'Stay still,' he said. 'Be quick.'

Aye. Right.

He moved again. This time, I struck out, deflected his wrist and twisted inside his arms to grip his left shoulder for balance. I brought my knee into his groin.

He wheezed and staggered back. '*Kurva Szar!*'

I danced away. Like a boxer. Float like a butterfly. He straightened. Shook his head in an admonishing fashion. 'Bad choice,' he said. '*Faszfej!*' Whatever the word meant, it wasn't a compliment.

'Aye, and fuck you, too.' Elegant response? I was under pressure. Oscar Wilde would lose his wit faced with a man who wanted to cut his skin to ribbons. The only thing worse than being talked about, after all, is being tortured to death.

He moved towards me again. The knife slashed out, I turned away too slow, felt a line of cold along my left arm. Looked down and saw blood. The sting came through clear and eye-opening.

The blood dripped.

'Appetiser,' the thug said. 'This room will paint with your blood.'

I held my arm, kept my distance. The thug

smiled. He could smell the blood. And the fear, too. He was a predator. Bako would have no need to persuade this man to the cause. He lived for blood and pain and fear. That much was in his eyes. They glinted in the dark like those of a wolf emerging from the trees in the dead of night, scenting wounded prey. He would have his flesh. And he would enjoy ripping it from the bones of a weaker, wounded animal.

Again, he lashed out with the blade. Moving fast for a big man. I didn't even realize he'd cut me again until I felt the soak of blood through my shirt. I stumbled and went down on my knees. He loomed over me. 'Now we have fun.'

I had been hurt before. But I'd never felt so alone. Perhaps because in the bad old days I'd already come to think of myself as a dead man walking; wearing my despair and loneliness like a favourite shirt, covered up by melancholy and self-pity. The last few years I had found myself again, rediscovered something of the person I had been. Thinking maybe I could build myself a normal kind of life.

But now my life would end here, in an anonymous and empty room.

Maybe that was fitting.

I used to read old noir novels. My dad's collection. Thousands of books with painted covers he'd bought on the cheap growing up, and later in second-hand stores. Authors like David Goodis, Jim Thompson. Books with characters whose lives spiralled around them no matter how much they tried to save themselves.

Noir wasn't just a literary style. It was a reflection of the world.

I closed my eyes.

There was a noise. Distant but audible. The sound of something crashing. Voices yelling.

I waited for the knife.

Got the sound of gunfire.

Forty-Four

I took deep breaths. In and out. The paramedic checked his instruments. Told me I was doing good. I'd be dizzy for a while, though, and he recommended a check-up at the hospital. I didn't argue. I was nauseous and light-headed.

Susan climbed in the ambulance, asked the guy to give us a moment. He gave her a look I didn't quite understand before climbing out.

I cleared my throat. Susan sat beside me. Held my hand. I let it stay limp.

'Well, this is fucked,' she said.

I almost laughed. Susan never sounded right swearing. Some people just don't have that kind of voice. She could threaten you with the most polite words.

I said, 'Aye. Fucked. All the way.'

'We got the car's plates from CCTV footage at the safe house. Tracked them through the city through cameras. Two streets away we lost them.'

'And, what, you just figured you'd knock on doors until you got the right one?'

'Frightened a lot of blue-rinsed old dears.'

'I'll bet you did.'

She squeezed my hand. 'I'm sorry.'

'For?'

'You wouldn't be here if it wasn't for me. When Griggs asked me to get involved with his pet project, I saw a way of getting back at the men who ruined my father's life.'

'And you figured I'd be on the same page?' Or, did she mean that I was one of those men?

'I didn't even think, Steed. Things between us had got strange. I wasn't . . . you and me . . .'

'Aye, when were things ever normal between us?'

We both fell silent again.

She said, 'Griggs has been suspended.'

'Oh?'

'Internal allegations of rogue operations and professional misconduct.'

'Who blew the whistle?'

'It's a sensitive investigation. Need to know.'

'Well there's a shock,' I said. I closed my eyes, exhaled long and slow. I was tired. The adrenaline burst from earlier was slowing. I could feel sleep stealing towards me.

Forty-Five

Two days later, a woman by the name of Gail Mitchell met me in an interview room on the second floor of FHQ. Maybe five-five, blonde hair cut to just above her shoulders, a no-nonsense kind of attitude. Soft, educated Glasgow accent. Shook my hand when I entered the room, said I was looking well and that maybe I should sit down. She was a good liar, even managed not to look at the stitches on my face.

When I sat down, I did it slowly. My muscles ached every time I moved. I could feel old injuries I'd almost forgotten re-establishing their presence.

'I want to talk to you about Sandy Griggs.'

Of course she did. Discipline and Complaints. Always Discipline and Complaints. Acting like your best friend when they wanted something from you.

'What about Griggs?'

'He reached out to you for assistance in an illegal investigation.'

'I believe it was unauthorized rather than necessarily illegal,' I said. 'And he didn't tell me that at the time. He's been running this one over a year. And this is the first time anyone has noticed? What did they think he was doing with his days?'

Mitchell ignored me. Maybe figuring I had every right to be pissed off. Maybe just not giving a toss. 'Not only did he fail to inform his superiors of the investigation, but the methods employed were questionable at best.'

'Isn't that always the way with undercover ops?' I said.

'Maybe. You have much experience?'

'Not really.'

'I do.' She let that one hang for a moment. Then: 'Tell me how Griggs reached out to you.'

217

'With a closed fist.' That earned me what might have been a smile. Or possibly indigestion. Either way, Mitchell lost the expression fast, and stayed quiet until I expanded on my answer. She wasn't here to make friends. She just wanted the truth.

I told her about how Griggs had approached me at a low point. How he manipulated my past mistakes so that I had no choice but to say yes to his proposal. I explained that Griggs had become increasingly monomaniacal over the course of our working together. 'He doesn't just want to arrest David Burns. He wants to crucify the man.'

Mitchell listened to my story dispassionately. Occasionally asked for clarification. But mostly she just let me talk. And I wanted to talk. To tell someone what had happened. All these months of keeping silent, I couldn't help but let it out.

By the time I was finished, I was exhausted. Short of breath. Taking in gulps of air between sentences.

Mitchell offered me a glass of water.

We sat there for a moment. No words. Nothing.

Finally 'I'm sorry. For everything that's happened. We will do our best to show that none of this was your idea. You were sucked into another man's private vendetta. You had no choice in your actions.'

Oh, she didn't know the half of it.

'So what happens now?'

Just a moment's hesitation. So I answered the question for her: 'I act like nothing's happened? And you do your thing?'

'There are procedures.'

'There are always procedures.'

'We need to substantiate—'

I shook my head. 'Save it. Really, I know the song. Every note.'

'You've been patient this long. Just a while longer. Work with us. We can fix this.'

'And if Griggs calls me?'

'Which we both know he will. If that happens, call me. We go from there.'

'Aye?'

'Right now, Griggs is paranoid. He knows that he's been running an illegal operation. And by now he has to have figured out he's been dropped in it. He's smart. Off the charts, really. One of the reasons the SCDEA snapped him up. His only hope right now is that you and Susan still believe every word he's told you. Or that you're both scared enough of what he knows to continue working with him.'

'Just tell me one thing.'

'Sure.'

'What is Griggs's issue with the old man? What started all of this?'

Mitchell shook her head. 'Now that's a story,' she said.

Forty-Six

2006.

I was still in uniform. Still awkward. Unsure of what I really wanted from the job. Beat work and clean up jobs were the order of the day.

In the canteen, drinking black coffee, pushing through one of those shifts that never seemed to end, a hand on my shoulder. 'McNee, right? You're up. With me.'

The hand of a senior detective. The hand of God. Selecting me and three other uniforms. More chance than design, I'd realize in retrospect. In our eyes, Griggs was righteous. Heroic. Some of the girls figured he looked like David Caruso. The cool David Caruso of *CSI: Miami*, not the washed-out would-be movie star he had almost become after quitting *NYPD Blue*.

God handed down skut work. I found myself standing outside a door, making sure only SOCOs and detectives accessed the scene. A murder, of course. Not that I got to see much of it. Just a corridor. An anonymous corridor in an anonymous building.

We all start somewhere. That was what I told myself.

What I remember was some guy arriving at the door, telling me he had access. Same age as Griggs. Smaller. Hard around the edges. Kind of look you'd figure life hadn't been easy on him. Bags under the eyes. Leather jacket worn tight like armour. A stare with the intensity of a live power socket. I didn't want to let him in. But Griggs told me this guy was central to the case.

Turned out the guy was an investigator. An old friend of Griggs. The two of them took over the scene. Cutting through standard protocol. What amazed me at the time: everyone just accepting the fact. As though men like Griggs could simply work to their own rules. But while Griggs was the man everyone respected, it was the guy in the leather jacket who seemed to call the shots. Griggs trusted him completely. Maybe more than some of his brother police. That stung a little, I guess. Looking back on it, I'd been uncomfortable with the idea of a senior detective breaking procedure in such a way. Back then, I'd believed utterly in the structure of the police, in the work that we did. It would take several years, and becoming a victim myself, to disillusion me to the point of walking away from it all.

Griggs had been a hero that day. The murder, linked to a conspiracy, sent down a dealer named Mick the Mick. Mick, who would later come back into my life as the trigger man in the murder of DCI Ernie Bright.

So what happened?

How did Griggs go from God to some lesser demon?

How did he wind up going from the man I admired, to the man who was responsible for screwing up my life so completely?

What happened?

Forty-Seven

Mitchell wasn't so sure herself what happened to Griggs. She had an idea, but couldn't prove anything. A few things had happened to Griggs during his last few years with Tayside that might explain the changes in his behaviour.

Starting with the charges brought against him for police brutality.

'The accusations were nonsense. Griggs was an outstanding officer. A force of moral constancy. Ask me five or six years – even five or six weeks – ago for a man who embodied the ideals of the Scottish police force, and I'd have said Sandy Griggs.'

Following the incident – Griggs had been set up by a local politician with a grudge – Griggs continued his career with enthusiasm and determination. Occasionally, he skated close to the edge of acceptable conduct, but he always did the right thing. Never once led D&C to believe he was anything other than a dedicated and upstanding officer. His flaws were human. Relatable. Understandable.

When he joined the SCDEA, Griggs had been a young hotshot. He had proved himself on the street. They expected great things from him on a national level. But something got in the way. He developed an obsession with a particular Dundee criminal: David Burns.

'Do you know what started it?' I asked.

Mitchell hesitated before answering. She played for time by rubbing her right hand along the back of her neck, as though massaging the answer out of herself. 'A number of things. But mostly . . . Griggs made a connection between the man who tried to frame him all those years ago and Burns. It was a connection the SCDEA had been aware of for some time, but Griggs had been kept in the dark.'

'Why?'

'The politician in question was . . . well, he was involved in some less than salubrious hobbies . . .'

'Sex?'

'What are the two things that catch most folk out?'

'Sex and drugs.'

'Rock and roll comes a distant third. But, aye. Sex. He was . . .' She didn't quite know how to put it. Her impassive expression collapsed for a moment. Why bother to hide her disgust? 'He liked to get his privates out in public places. Griggs caught him doing it once, and the bastard never got over the humiliation. But that was just the start. The man had a thing for working girls, too. And, well, he got caught out again. But this time, Griggs had nothing to do with it.'

David Burns's honey traps were notorious. The stuff of station-gossip legend. Which always struck me as odd, given that the old man was as conservative as they come when it came to sex. Definitely a one-woman man. He was never seen in any of the dancing clubs he owned, never had a bit on the side, never strayed from Mary. He pumped money into gentlemen's clubs, but never ever set foot inside one. Often said he didn't care to know what went on in such places. Private lives, he said, should remain private.

Of course, hypocrisy could have been the old man's middle name. And he was perfectly willing to prey on others' predilections.

'Griggs had been working on a few local dealers. These men were connected to Burns. The old man wanted revenge. Used the politician to set up the sting with Griggs.'

'But Griggs never figured that part out.'

'No. Not at first. The councillor never talked about it, either. He kept quiet, did his time for attempting to pervert the course of justice. Never once mentioned Burns.'

'But someone at SCDEA knew.'

'Yes.'

'And Griggs found out?'

'We think he found out before applying for the transfer. Maybe thought joining the Agency was his best crack at getting one over on Burns.'

'Except he never got the chance . . .'

'Priorities change.'

'Anti-terror?'

'Among other things, yes.'

Burns had never been one for political causes. Rumour was he'd once attended a meeting with a high level member of the Provisional IRA – who had been looking to the old man for supply of weapons – simply to tell the man to 'Kiss my arse'. Burns's family were Catholic Irish originally, two generations removed from the old man himself, but he wouldn't ally himself with anyone whose methods he disagreed with. Burns wasn't averse to violence, but only against those who brought it on themselves. Either by getting in his way or getting in over their head. He saw those with addictions or perversions as making conscious decisions. Violence against people who knew what they were doing was fine. But Burns could never handle violence that involved innocents – or people who Burns could classify as innocent – no matter how just or unjust the cause. If you could be called a terrorist, you would get no help from the old man.

I could see, then, why the SCDEA might allow their focus on Burns to drop. The new political climate was international. Hollywood blockbuster scale. The new lords and masters didn't care so much about men like Burns: men who only fought for small land grabs, whose power was limited locally. The SCDEA and the Government wanted the public to see the kind of results that looked good on twenty-four-hour rolling news channels. Homegrown gangsters were old news. They were safe, even. Movies like *Lock, Stock*, along with the canonization of men like Ronnie Biggs had ensured that the public were no longer concerned about organized crime that operated to the old rules. There was something quaint about men like Burns when compared to the kind of brutal terrorism that started to flood our consciousness.

If Griggs had transferred specifically to stick the boot into the old man, then it made sense that he would be pissed off when the priorities shifted so fast. But there's a difference between that, and taking your campaign to a whole other level in the way Griggs had done.

What made it so personal?

'The only person who could answer that would be Griggs himself.'

'And?'

'And we don't know where he is. He's not at home. He's not at the hotel room Bright told us he'd be staying at. He's vanished.'

'Does he know you want to talk to him?'

'Do I look like I just started at this job?'

'Hard to say.'

'You've already taken down one corrupt copper. Maybe two.'

'No,' I said. 'Griggs isn't corrupt. Stupid. Misguided. Maybe just blind because he's angry. But not corrupt. He's not a bad man.'

'You know what he did to you.'

'I know what I did to myself. Griggs took advantage of my weaknesses. And he played a blinder by poking holes in the James Robertson case.'

'Where you shot a man in self-defence?'

'Killed him. Deliberately. And covered up the facts.'

'You realize what you're saying?'

'Yes, I do. What I did, I did out of anger. Because I had no choice. But I lied about certain facts.' Just saying it made my chest feel easier. Like a metal band that had been placed across it for the last five years had suddenly been removed.

'The second gun belonged to you?'

'In a manner of speaking. Someone else put it in my hand.'

Mitchell nodded. 'David Burns.'

'Yes.'

'Why?'

'Because, like Griggs, he saw something in me that he could use.'

'The anger.'

'Yes.'

'Were you drinking?'

'What?'

'At the time you shot and killed a man, were you drinking? You were grieving the loss of your

226

fiancée. You had a reputation as a man with a hair trigger temper. So I have to wonder if you were drinking. Excessively.'

I shook my head. 'No more than most folks.'

'And what does that mean?'

'Exactly what I said. I drank. No more or less than I do now.'

She put her hands on the table, fingers locked together. Leaned in. Serious. Made me think of the force-appointed psychologist I had seen after my suspension for assaulting a senior officer. 'So how did you get through what happened?'

'Anger. Hate.'

'I see.'

I nodded.

She said, 'During that period, by all accounts, you exhibited the behaviour of an alcoholic. Or at least a depressive.'

'Maybe. Can you blame me?'

'But you didn't drink.'

'Aye, I don't like to be predictable.'

'I guess not.'

'So tell me what happens now.'

'Your confession gets swept under the rug. The situation was . . . extreme. And the matter resolved itself. I don't want any more paperwork than I'm already facing.'

'Tell that to DI Kellen.'

She smiled. Tight lips and cold eyes. 'I might.'

'Won't change her mind. Might make her more determined.'

'Maybe. Maybe not. But my point, Mr McNee, is that there are degrees of sin. And they can be measured by intent.'

'Philosophical for Discipline and Complaints.'
'We're smarter than people give us credit for.'
I didn't argue with her.
What was there left to say?

Forty-Eight

My fifth cup of weak coffee. My third hour in a small room with only my reflection for company.

The door opened. Susan came in. I stood up, not sure how to greet her. She did the hard work. Wrapped her arms round me and pressed her head against my chest.

When she pulled back, she looked at me with her head cocked to one side and said, 'Do you think it's us?'

'What?'

'Every time our paths cross, things get messed up.'

'That's depressing.'

'Guess so.'

We stood in silence for a moment.

She said, 'Or maybe it's just me.'

'No. Really. It's not.'

She smiled. We sat down, pulling the chairs out from the table so that there was nothing between us. She said, 'I can't help feeling this is my fault. I'm the one got you into this.'

'One way or another, Griggs would have got what he wanted.'

'I'm an idiot.'

'No. He promised you the one thing you wanted.'

She nodded. 'He lied to me. Told me that Burns had been responsible for my father's death, that none of this would have happened if the old man hadn't got into his stupid feud with a crooked cop. That was wrong. Burns wasn't responsible. Not really. He wasn't the one who forced my dad into the position of working undercover.'

I had to wonder what magic Griggs had worked on Ernie. Or whether Ernie had simply allowed himself to become a stooge. Wherever Griggs's obsession came from, Ernie's had to have been greater. After all, the DCI had been trying to pin down Burns for years. Had been forced into a situation where Burns was the devil he knew back in the nineties. And then, when the truce was cancelled by brass, he watched time and again as the law failed to crack down on a man who flouted it so easily.

Maybe all Griggs had to do was ask Ernie. Maybe that had been enough.

But I didn't say any of this. Not to Susan. She had to have the same thoughts. But we all lie to ourselves about the people we love. Assign them higher motivations than they deserve. Jump through hoops to excuse behaviour from them that we might deplore in others.

Susan and I sat in silence for a while.

Comfortable.

She was the only person in the world could make me feel that way.

Something to count against what she had noted

earlier: that whenever we were together, things tended to go to shite.

Forty-Nine

DS Ewan 'Sooty' Soutar popped his shaved head round the door and told us we were being moved elsewhere. 'Orders from above.'

'You're babysitting? Who'd you piss off?'

Sooty didn't respond, just shook his head and waited for us to stand. As I moved past her, Susan's hand brushed against mine. A momentary touch, but comforting. Filled with a kind of promise I couldn't put into words.

We left FHQ through the front entrance, climbed into Sooty's unmarked. Susan took the front seat. I climbed in the back. Made sense. Susan was still a cop with a reputation. I was just an arsehole with seemingly limitless second chances.

Sooty drove us down through the centre. We hit the mess of roadworks that were the first stages of the city's regeneration. Every time you came down, the layout changed subtly. More than once, I'd found myself accidentally heading over the bridge. And it seemed no different. But he didn't seem to care. Halfway across, I realized that it wasn't a mistake. We were crossing the bridge.

I leaned forward. 'Mind telling us where we're going?'

Sooty didn't say much. I saw his face in the

rear view mirror. Uncomfortable. He was a direct man. Lying didn't come easy. In interrogation, he opted for the straightforward approach, relied on his size to get a confession. He never beat anyone. But the idea that he might was a powerful, psychological weapon.

Of course, physical intimidation aside, he couldn't bluff to save his life. I'd learned that much during off-duty hands of poker back in the good old days, when we were friends by virtue of wearing the same uniform.

He pulled into the car park across the other side of the water. Same place where Griggs and I used to park parallel for face-to-face meets. Sure enough, I recognized the only other car waiting for us.

'What the fuck?' Susan said.

Sooty couldn't look at us.

'You know he's under investigation?'

'No one told me anything. I just know he's SCDEA and he wants to talk to you.' But there was a hesitation there. Maybe no one had told him anything, but he still knew the situation was dodgy.

'My arse,' Susan said. 'You know Sandy. You two go back . . .'

'He's doing the right thing. It's the bloody system that's . . .' His face was reddening. Frustration. Stuck between friendship and the job. He'd always told me that I didn't know which side I was on. His world was simple: black and white. Right and wrong. He knew where his loyalties lay. Except that in that one moment, he didn't. Because there was no right or wrong that

231

matched up to what he understood. His friend and his superior was in the wrong. But because he believed so utterly on both things, he couldn't accept that.

I couldn't help myself. I laughed.

He gripped the steering wheel so that his knuckles whitened. His jaw went tight. He spoke through a mouth that didn't want to move. 'Tell me you've always been in the right, McNee. Tell me how you were always morally fucking upright. Aye, Sandy's made some mistakes, but . . .'

'Last time I made a mistake like he did, you tried to break my neck.' Like I said, Sooty could be direct. And when something offended him personally – and it was the rare person I couldn't offend personally – he tended to get physical.

This time, he didn't say anything. Or do anything. He was aware of his own hypocrisy. But couldn't do anything about it. Not now.

I shook my head. Got out of the car.

Fifty

Griggs met me halfway. We stopped as though there was an invisible barrier between us. The wind cut sharp. Whipped against my skin like branches of a birch tree. I dug my hands deep into my jacket pockets.

'You fuck,' I said.

'Tell me you wouldn't do anything to put him away, the things he's done.'

'I'd have given my patsy a choice. I wouldn't have forced him into—'

'I didn't think you'd resist.' There was some regret there, sneaking in just below the words. As though he knew he'd done wrong. Didn't want to admit it.

'I was putting my life back together. I was so fucking close. And then you came along.'

'Back together? Didn't look so hot to me. Or Susan.' His body language was wrong. His shoulders were drooped. He had difficulty looking into my eyes. He wanted to be in control, but he couldn't manage it. Because he could see his world falling apart. All the certainties he'd had were gone. He was no longer in control.

I could sense Susan behind me. She must have wanted to speak. But didn't say a word. Because she knew he was trying to provoke her? Or because she knew he had a point?

Maybe she knew that this conversation was about me and Griggs. Her own words would come later.

I said, 'So you thought you'd help me find my sense of purpose?'

'Something like that.'

'And when I didn't play along, you decided the only thing left to do was to manipulate me? Make sure I had no choice but to do what you wanted?'

'Desperate times.'

'Desperate? Like fuck, Griggs. So what did all of this achieve? Aside from monumentally screwing up both our lives? Tell me?'

'We rattled him. The old man's on the ropes.

Ready to give up. He knows he's past it. He knows the evidence is stacked. He knows—'

'—Does it matter to you how many people are going to die? Needlessly? The old man's gone to war. Against a psychopath who wouldn't think twice about killing anyone who got in his way.'

Susan couldn't take it anymore. She couldn't keep quiet. 'Jesus, Sandy! All of this . . . all you think you achieved . . . it doesn't mean anything! The evidence you gained was procured by illegal methods. Your undercover operation was never sanctioned. Everything you did undermines the legitimacy of your intentions.'

Griggs nodded. I wondered how long he'd been saddled with that knowledge. He can't have started this knowing that he was in the wrong. He had to have blinded himself with the zeal of the righteous. By the time he realized that what he was doing was morally and legally compromised, he must have also realized there was no way back. He was committed.

Never start something you can't finish.

One of the first things my dad had taught me.

Wonder who taught Griggs that. Or whether he learned that lesson the hard way.

I looked at him. Saw something like I used to see looking in the mirror. A man who knew that what he was doing was wrong. Who knew that he was damned but still continued because he didn't know how to do anything else.

A man obsessed.

Looking for a revenge he could never have.

I said, 'This isn't about Burns setting you up all those years ago, is it? This isn't about his empire stretching beyond the control of the police. This isn't political. This is personal.'

He nodded. Finally looked at me head on.

I said, 'So tell me.'

Fifty-One

2007.

Another junkie. Another death. Same old story. Repeated so many times, it was easy to stop caring about each individual case.

This one was found face down in a big pile of bin bags at the rear end of a housing complex. Those who found her didn't know which smell was worse: the rotting garbage or the rotting corpse.

Her death was unremarkable as these things go. An OD. Shooting up at the rear of the property, collapsing among the bags. Her last desperate breaths taking in the scents of rotting fruit and decomposing meat. A sad end to a sad life. But in the grand scheme, no better or worse than most.

The girl had a sheet stretching back decades. Drug addiction. Prostitution. Debts out of her eyeballs. Both to banks and other unregulated institutions. She was homeless in an on and off fashion. She sold the *Big Issue* for three months, working the pitch on Union Street, harassing the punters heading for the bookstore, sometimes getting a gentle warning from the community officers for being overly aggressive with her sales patter. Eventually she got booted from the programme for habitually and consistently selling while high.

There are rules, after all. Helping the homeless to help themselves. Not just helping the homeless for nothing.

She didn't get that, really. Expected just another charity she could try and scam.

Banned from the *Issue*, she turned tricks, same way she had when she was new to the scene. Back then she'd been heroin chic, still with that little-girl-lost appeal. But years pumping powder left her looking old before her time. Bone thin, plaster white, reminding any potential punters of death more than lust. Slowing hearts more than speeding them up. Her whining pitch didn't help matters, like she was begging folk for a fuck rather than offering an illicit thrill.

It didn't work out. So she escaped like she always did.

Got high. Turned on. Tuned in. Dropped out one last and final time. Right on top of Tesco Value meals and crushed cans of lager.

The cops worked the scene with dutiful respect for the dead. But no one mourned her passing. Her name passed before the eyes of so many people who just shrugged and accepted her death as part of the cycle of things. It wasn't that these people didn't care. It was that the weight of the things they saw every day was so much greater than the death of a person who seemed to have done little to try and save themselves. To them, the dead girl seemed to have been seeking death more than living life.

And then her name passed before Sandy Griggs.

The Burns project was winding down. Griggs had tried to fight it, but the powers that be were insisting that the old man and his operations could no longer be classed a priority. Griggs and a few others continued to work the old man's files. They would do so until someone told them to stop. They had feelers out on the streets and in the police station. They read the official reports. Kept an eye on the old man. His suppliers. Their customers.

Any business relating to Burns came to them. And finally, it simply came to Griggs. The last man standing. The last man with the energy to care about an operation no one wanted any more.

The man who dealt to the dead girl went by the name of Damon Oliver. He was thirty-three years old, had a business degree and was working off a big debt to one of the old man's enforcers. At the same time, he was chancing his arm by working as a police informant. Figuring he could play both sides against each other. In his head, Oliver was the smartest guy in the room. It was the kind of lie people tell themselves so they don't just give up.

Hence why, when the girl died, Oliver held up his hands and said, 'The batch was good. It was her system that was fucked, couldn't handle it.' Figuring he had to get ahead of this one before they thought she was violating the terms of his agreement with the cops. It was a double bind, but in Oliver's mind, he wasn't the one at fault.

Oliver supplied the drugs.

Oliver was in hock to David Burns.

The girl's name was CeeCee McKenzie. She kept her married name even after the divorce. Because it embarrassed her brother. Her brother who was a cop.

She wasn't born CeeCee. She was born Catherine.

Catherine Griggs.

Fifty-Two

We stood by the barriers and looked out across the Tay to the city's lights. There was something beautiful about this particular view of the city. It was easy to laugh about Dundee, but at night, from across the water, the lights had a strange, translucent quality of hope.

My dad used to say that if you looked at the city from across the water you might be fooled into admiring the place. Speaking the way only someone who truly loves and understands a place can. He was a native, had seen the city through good and bad and never left, despite his moaning and his stated desires to travel to far off places. He could badmouth the place all he wanted because he still loved it, saw beneath all of that cynicism to the very heart of the place.

Griggs, looking across at those lights, said, 'CeeCee. I think she heard the name on TV once, thought it sounded exotic. I told her it just sounded daft. Maybe that was my mistake. Maybe that was the turning point. Just one wrong word.

238

One moment. But then again . . .' He shook his head. He wasn't really talking to me any more. He was inside his own head. Thinking about things he'd spent a long time trying to forget. 'I read a study, years ago, about children from abusive relationships and the ways that they wind up. They have a lot in common with children of alcoholics. More often than not, you know, there's an overlap . Anyway, seems they wind up either vowing never to allow themselves to become that way, becoming campaigners for an end to such behaviour or . . .'

'. . . or they reflect their parent's behaviour.'

He looked at me as though only just remembering I was there. Turning his head just enough so that he could get a look at my face, maybe trying to figure out if I knew more than I was letting on. He'd have to keep wondering.

After a moment, he looked away again, back across the water. 'CeeCee and I both witnessed what happened between our parents. It wasn't pleasant. It ended badly. I'm sure you know.'

'As much as I need to.'

He smiled at that. Humourless. Lips pressed tight together so that the blood rushed away from them. 'She was too young to really process what was happening. But I knew. Tried to fight back. But I was always too small, too young, too power-less . . .' He stopped himself there, as though realizing that he was oversharing. 'And then . . . well, you know what happened.'

As much as the official reports would say, of course. Some of the records were still sealed.

'Catherine . . . CeeCee . . . was still too young

239

to grasp the truth. Maybe that's what messed her up. Didn't help that they sent us to separate foster homes. I was her brother. I was supposed to protect her. How could I when they tore us apart like that?'

Griggs had always been a man with a strong sense of responsibility. A man of honour. He did not lie, cheat, break his word. Not without good reason. I had wondered what changed that about him, but now I understood. He had not changed, but he had lost his focus. Allowed personal feelings to overshadow larger responsibilities.

'We lost track of each other. We would write, but over time, while I wrote every week, her letters became infrequent. Sloppy. She was thirteen or fourteen, when she stopped the letters completely. She'd tried to escape from the foster homes they were sending her to. Fallen into bad company. Had this boyfriend a few years older who'd discovered the joys of dealing pot. The guy had big ambitions. You know, wanted to be like Johnny Depp in *Blow*. Guess he didn't see the end of that one, because he wound up in Perth prison and then he wound up dead. Killed over a measly two hundred quid.'

'CeeCee told you that?'

'No. I didn't know what was going on with her. But the people I was staying with at the time knew what she meant to me, kept what tabs they could on her. When they told me, it was three weeks after he was pronounced, and I could see in their faces that keeping this from me had been difficult. Guess they didn't know what to tell me. How to tell me. How do you tell a

240

sixteen-year-old kid that his sister's boyfriend got her hooked on drugs, wound up dead in prison and left her all alone in the world? And how do you tell that kid that you're sorry, there's nothing you can do? The system won't allow you to interfere.'

'What happened to CeeCee?'

'Vanished. In the wind. Not for the first time, but this time no one was able to trace her. It was four years before she contacted me again. Showed up at my house, in fact.'

'Where had she been?'

'Here and there. I could piece some of it together. I was a copper, then. Had contacts. Did a little out of hours investigation. She stayed in the city. Never thought about moving on. Mostly squats and communes. You know, the kind of thing might be exciting for a while when you're young, but fucks you if you don't get out in time. When she came to my door – I don't know how she tracked me down – she was strung out on all kinds of shit, looking for a hand-out. Maybe just so she could keep getting high. Or maybe she really did want a fresh start. What I offered her was a place to stay and a chance to find some work. Get clean, you know. Some of the outreach workers I knew could have helped. I just wanted my old sister back. Calling her CeeCee, the way she wanted, she just didn't seem like my sister.'

'Did she accept the offer?'

'She stayed on my couch for three days. Then ripped off some of mum's old jewellery I had stored away, and bolted. It hurt, really. Not losing the jewellery. But the idea that she would take advantage of me, that maybe she'd planned it that way. Sponge off her brother until she could figure out the next scam. I felt like an idiot for loving her, and that's what hurt.'

I never had brothers or sisters. Growing up it had been me, Mum and Dad. I had never quite understood that odd bond that exists between siblings. Particularly distanced ones. Never quite got how you could love someone at the same time as you can hate who they might become. Knowing siblings was like knowing that your friends are having a party and they might try and invite you, but you still wind up outside a dirt-smudged window, looking in and trying to see what a great time they're having.

'That was it. She was gone, then. I had to let her go, know that she would find her own way. Maybe I always knew she'd wind up the way she did. You'd have to be blind, deaf and dumb not to figure it out. And even then you'd still have to not be paying attention. All the same, men like Burns, men who let shit flood the streets, who have no thoughts for the consequences of what they do . . .'

'Your sister always had a choice.'

'You've never known addiction,' he said. 'Choice doesn't really enter into it. That's the kicker. The heart-breaking thing. That someone can want to quit but the urge to do whatever it is that's destroying them over-rides their own self-preservation. If they can stay away from triggers, maybe they have a chance, but when those triggers are around them every day or within reach, then it's so damn easy to slide and . . .'

He stopped talking. Took a deep breath. 'She died, and there was no one to blame. Not even the fucking dealer.'

The problem with police work is that you see the bigger picture. How things come to be the way they are. You understand the network that grows around drug dealers. You view crime from the top down, seeing not just the street level impact of crimes, but the network of events that leads to one isolated act of violence or neglect. You can't just blame the dealer. You blame the money. And you blame the money men. And you know that there are some people you just can't touch no matter how hard you try.

Men like David Burns.

The root cause of a criminal act is often utterly isolated and removed from the act itself. Like a blood-soaked version of the old game, Six Degrees of Kevin Bacon.

'I figured you would know what it's like. Knowing that someone out there destroyed something you love. Being unable to do a damn thing about it. They never found the driver of that car, McNee. You never knew who killed your fiancée. Just that it happened. I was already gone when she died. Working out of the Glasgow office. But you know the police: word travels. I heard about what happened. I felt for you. I really did. And I guess that hung around the back of my mind, because it was your name that came to mind when I needed a new way to get to the old man.'

He was right. I understood Griggs's obsession. Better than most. We were the same. In so many ways.

Except, what he failed to understand: I had moved past my despair and my need for revenge. Perhaps because at some point I finally accepted that I would never find the person responsible for the accident. That they were a ghost; a half-glimpsed thing that you could never say for sure had ever really been there.

Griggs was reminded every day of his sister's death. And of the man he knew was to blame. He had the means and the opportunity to gain his revenge. He had taken it. Who wouldn't have?

He came so close. He had the bastard in his sights. Only for his opportunity to be snatched away. By men in suits. By changing political winds.

How would I have felt?

What would I have done?

Whatever it took.

I wouldn't have cared about the inconvenience to other people. Not back when my wounds were fresh and raw.

I said, 'So what happens now?'

'It's over, right?' His shoulders were slumped. His words came out like an extended sigh.

'Maybe you can work a deal.'

He snorted. 'I've seen what happens to coppers who make deals with D&C. It's never pleasant.'

'So what else can you do?'

He nodded. 'What else can I do?' He stretched, as though he was tired. And maybe he was. Everything he had been through had come crashing down around him. He couldn't rebuild. He couldn't walk away. He had to live with the consequences. One way or another. 'Maybe you're right. I should just turn myself in. Maybe someone else will bring him in. We have a case.'

'They've not forgotten about him.'

'He's too old for prison. Get a slap on the wrist, maybe a cushy retirement home.'

'Think he wants to go out like that? He sees himself as an old cowboy. Wants to die with his boots on. I know he tells Mary different, but that's the truth. He thinks the best way to die is while he's still in the game. Taking him out of it, letting him die like any other old codger, maybe that's the best punishment there is for a man like Burns.'

'Maybe. Maybe.'

I said, 'Whatever happens, the war is over. The Zombie is in prison.'

'Normality resumes.'

'It's always the way.'

The wind chilled a little. I said, 'It's time to go. Time to end this.'

'You still have the phone?'

I nodded. 'Who paid for it?'

'SCDEA. A little creative accountancy.' He shook his head. 'That's going to count against me, too. The fuckers, they'll come at me with everything.'

'You pays your money . . .'

'You takes your chances. Aye, aye, aye. Who'd have thought it would come to this?'

'You can bounce back.' Even I didn't believe me.

'You think?'

He rolled his head as though getting rid of a

245

kink in his neck. Extended his hand. I took it. His long fingers wrapped around mine, like tightening cords of rope.

He pulled me in, slammed his knee into my belly. Fast. Brutal. Unexpected. No chance to brace myself.

I doubled. He grabbed my hair and flung me back. I was off balance, had no choice but to follow the momentum. I landed awkward, hit something hard. No pain. Just a dull sensation at the back of my skull and a feeling like the world was a badly edited film where the frames were starting to stutter.

I rolled over.

He started to go through my pockets.

Maybe I said something.

Maybe I was already gone.

Fifty-Three

First thing I noticed: the pain was sharp. At the back of my skull. Insistent. Someone gently scraping a razor across bone. My hair was thickly matted with blood. I could feel its slowly spreading warmth.

I opened my eyes. Saw Susan, looking down at me. 'It's a habit,' she said. 'People punching hell out of you.'

'Love you, too.'

She reacted like she'd caught her finger in a mousetrap. But her recovery was fast as she tried

246

for a grin: 'Oh, aye, you've got some of the old brain-shake, then?'

I tried to sit up. There was a jacket beneath my head to make up for the lack of pillow, but I could feel the gravel beneath me. I was nauseous, wondered if I should even be trying to move.

Concussion.

A condition I'd become familiar with over the last few years. We were getting to be friends.

'Griggs?'

'Aye,' said Sooty. Standing close, but facing away, arms folded. Gaze on the distance, as though he could see something that wasn't quite in focus. Whatever it was, he didn't look too happy about it. 'Prick took off.' He turned to look at me. 'None of the told-you-so's, right?'

'Aye,' I said. 'Right.'

He didn't crack a smile. Just shook his head. If you couldn't trust a rogue SCDEA agent, who could you trust these days?

I sat up. Slowly. Tried not to touch the back of my head. Susan, crouched beside me, placed her hands on my shoulders as though afraid I'd just go right back over.

McNee might wobble, but he doesn't fall down. Not when it matters.

When I went down, Griggs had searched my pockets. I remembered that much before I shut down completely. What had he been looking for? I patted down my jacket. Trying to think what the hell it was that he would want from me.

'Fucksakes!'

'Steed?'

'You know you said you always chose the

247

wrong fucking men? Aye, well, this one was a right catch and no fucking mistake.'

She didn't say anything.

I felt heat rise to my face. Burning.

'I'm sorry. I . . .' Was there any point saying anything? The damage was done. 'Look, Griggs knows he's made a mistake. The trouble is, I think he believes there's no way out, now. He's started, so he'll finish. And I'm worried what that will mean for him.'

Susan said, 'Burns?'

I nodded. 'I need your phone. Please. I have to try and make this right.'

I didn't want this night to end in blood. There had been enough spilled over the years. Enough people had died. Just once, I wanted to try and make things better.

Susan passed me her phone. I dialled through to Burns's home number. No reply. 1571 cutting in after maybe twenty seconds.

No one at home?

Or already too late?

I said, 'Give me the keys,' talking to Sooty.

'No way. You're bleeding. That was a bastard of a knock to the head. We're waiting for the amb—'

'—Give me the fucking keys.'

Sooty looked ready to lamp me. But instead he threw his car keys towards at me. They arced high in the air. I almost let them drop. 'Take them,' he said, 'We're all buggered anyway. Right?'

Fifty-Four

I drove back across the bridge. The car was buffeted by strong cross-winds. My touch on the steering wheel was distant, as though the nerves in my hands were located some distance away from my body.

I'd taken a whack to the head. I shouldn't have been behind the wheel.

I'd had my share of knocks over the years. My body was scarred in places I never expected. My right hand couldn't close properly after someone had broken it. The limp I gained after the crash came and went, but on cold nights I still felt like my muscles were seizing up. They'd told me it was psychosomatic. I'd never been that convinced.

I was a mess. Always had been. One wrong blow would be all it took to completely fuck me up. And still I kept going.

I'd known it happen to a guy once. One of those cautionary tales that got bandied around at ABI conventions. The guy wasn't officially an eye. He'd been an ex-con who decided to get into the security business. In over his head. He worked mostly for bad people down in Manchester, would never have made it past ABI checks even if he'd wanted to. But the nature of our business has always meant that a number of people operate off the books. That's why the calls for official regulation had been so loud in recent years. Ours was a profession that needed to protect its reputation.

This guy – I think his name was Inglis, maybe, or perhaps I'm getting confused – was the Mr Bean of close protection. Wound up getting hit with a cricket bat, run over by a car, all kinds of crap. Finally, he suffered a massive stroke – he couldn't have been older than thirty or thirty-five – and lost all feeling on his left side. One too many beatings and a refusal to listen to his own body. Pushing himself beyond his own endurance. Not helped by a little codeine addiction, too, from what I gathered. I hadn't gone that far, but all the same, my physical state was beginning to leave a little something to be desired. If I was a car, I'd be worried about passing my MOTs in the future.

Across the bridge, I slipped into the east-bound lane. My first port of call was Burns's home. Hoping I'd ring the doorbell, drag him out in his dressing gown. Would mean that, for once, I'd be on time.

The traffic was light. I drove past the new swimming pool, built on the site of the Old Borders building. Round the city centre, nothing seemed to stay still for long. The city was evolving, changing. Five or six years, it was going to be unrecognizable. And maybe that was the point. Dundee had been promising change for decades. Finally, that promise was, it seemed, being acted upon.

On the Arbroath Road, I heard sirens, pulled over to let the fire engines whip past me. And the police vans, too. Got a heavy feeling in my stomach. Once they were past, I broke the speed limits to keep up.

The burnt orange halo reminded me of bonfires from my youth. We'd head out to Balgay Park and watch the fireworks every fifth of November, wrapped up in heavy coats, heads warmed by woolly hats and hands toasted by clumsy gloves that made it difficult to hold sparklers properly.

For just a moment, I imagined that I could see a guy perched jauntily on the roof of the house. But it was simply shadows and the blurred edges of my vision combining to create an unpleasant illusion.

DI Duncan 'Donuts' was the first responder. When he saw me climbing out of the car, he shook his head, walked right over, held out a warning hand and said, 'Get to fuck, McNee.' He looked tired. In the flickering light of the fire, his skin was pale and washed out. He was going bald, his remaining strands of hair holding on to the dome of his head for dear life, slapped across like three dark scores on the surface of a bruised apple.

'Just tell me if there's anyone in there.'

'Best the lads can say, the house is empty. Surprised it's taken this long for anyone to try a stunt like this. Guess his rep's not what it was. Mind you, look at the company he keeps, aye?'

'Any clues as to—'

'You know you're the enemy these days?'

'Just because I do some private work for the old man doesn't mean . . .'

'I defended you a time or two,' the fat

detective said. He wiped his brow, sweating despite his distance from the burning house. Maybe it was just the few steps over the road to meet me that had exhausted him. I wondered how he ever passed his physicals. 'The last couple of years, I started to wonder if maybe we had you pegged wrong. And then you started working for him.'

I didn't have the breath to waste telling him how he had it all wrong. There wasn't time to argue.

I said, 'Do you have an idea who started this? I need to know if it was—'

'Oh, aye, the infamous fucking Zombie? That who you mean?' He laughed. 'McNee, you really need to keep the fuck up, eh?' He shook his head. 'Go home, you prick. Go home. Leave this shite to the professionals.'

Fifty-Five

Go home.

Except I knew one of the basic truths of life: you can never go home again.

If there had been no one in the house, then I had to wonder what Griggs was thinking. Had he finally lost it? He'd set the fire. Had to have been him. With Bako under arrest – although the way Donuts had laughed when I mentioned his name gave me pause for thought – Griggs was the only person with the balls to make such a direct move. This wasn't the cockroaches crawling out from the dark spaces. Not yet.

But why?

Was he sending a message?

Why take my phone if he wasn't going to use it? Didn't need that to set a fire.

He had to be trying to lure the old man out into the open. It's what I would have done: sent a text message from someone the old man trusted, arranged a meeting and then . . . well, done whatever it was I needed to do.

The fire was a puzzle, though. An unexpected kind of melodrama. It meant something. Perhaps cathartic. Cleansing in some way.

I remembered the way that Gemma Fairstead and Teale had talked about fire. Their thing had become sexual, but in the beginning, I had the feeling that the fire had been a release. A way of burning out their anger. Their frustration.

Was this what it meant to Griggs? In this moment, was he burning out all his frustration?

But what did he want, exactly? What was the end game? Where was all this leading?

A good investigator tries to think like their target. Attempts to understand their needs, wants, motivations.

What was Griggs thinking?

What would I be thinking if I were Griggs?

I would want revenge. I would want to see the old man pay for what he had done.

What did that mean?

That I wanted kill the old man? No. I could have done that at the house.

So, what?

David Burns had to suffer. And he had to know and understand what he had done to me.

How could I achieve that?

I'd need a place where we could be alone. Undisturbed.

Where?

Where would I go if I were Griggs?

It couldn't just be somewhere quiet. That was only part of the requirement. It needed to be somewhere with meaning. Somewhere where the old man could not escape his guilt and complicity in what had happened.

You can never go home again.

The phrase was echoing in my head. Why?

Home was family.

Family was what had started Griggs's vendetta. Forget the personal attacks Burns had made against Griggs. For a copper like Griggs that was business as usual. But CeeCee's death had made it personal.

CeeCee.

Found dead at the back of a council house. Discarded among the trash and detritus no one wanted to see.

CeeCee.

Griggs had wanted to protect her. Never had the chance. He didn't know who she had been, where she lived. All he knew of her was where she died.

That was all he had.

Where she died.

I knew where Griggs was. What he was planning.

I just hoped I wasn't too late.

Fifty-Six

I would only discover later what happened.

How Burns came when he got the message. Whether or not he knew he was walking into a trap, I'll never be sure. But he showed up. Alone. As though he really believed I was the one who'd contacted him.

Griggs watched him leave the house. He'd been parked across the street, watching the old man's house. Waiting for his moment. He let the other car pull away and waited for a few minutes before breaking into the house. Patient. He knew that if he rushed any of this, he risked blowing his last chance. He set the fire in the living room, and walked out of the house as though he had merely been visiting. None of the neighbours realized anything was wrong until the windows at the front blew open with the sheer force of the interior heat. Shards of hot glass rained down on what had once been the safest street in the city.

The old man's empire was crumbling. He was vulnerable. Two attacks in as many weeks. People were getting the message.

This was why Griggs had set the fire. A final humiliation.

Griggs sent a second text message to Burns:
Change of plans. Meet at new location. Security compromised.

Burns didn't recognize the new address. Why

would he? What would he have cared about an empty building where they once found the dead body of a drug-addicted girl whose life had ended before it even had a chance to begin?

He didn't know CeeCee's name. He wouldn't have cared anyway. Her choices had nothing to do with him.

Burns arrived at the new destination maybe ten minutes later. He climbed out of the car and looked around, maybe wondering why I had chosen this place to meet.

But he wasn't here to meet me.

And when he saw Griggs, he smiled.

It was nine years since CeeCee's corpse had been found at the rear of the property. The building had been empty for half that time. The doors were shuttered, the windows covered by metal grates to stop intruders and squatters from breaking in. Not that it made a difference. The pebble-dash walls were washed out by years of neglect. The front garden was overgrown. People dropped their rubbish among the tall grass as they passed by. Bottle shards and needles sparkled in the moonlight. The house had a grim kind of beauty.

I walked up to the main door. The padlock had been broken, the metal cover pushed aside. I pushed it further, let the long-dead house swallow me up. The hallway was dark. I blinked, my eyes adjusting to the dark. I began to distinguish silhouettes; enough to place the stairs leading up to the second level and the length of the corridor leading to the kitchen at the rear of the property.

Bile rose up the back of my throat. The world lurched, like a passenger liner caught in a sudden swell. I reached out to steady myself, my hand touching the cold, rough plaster of the walls.

'Hello? Griggs?' My voice seemed to crack. But I couldn't afford weakness. Once this was done, once this was finally over, I would seek medical attention. If it wasn't too late.

I had spent the last few years drawn inevitably to the broken places in the city; the remaining hangovers of decades of poverty that had afflicted the self-described City of Discovery. My life had not moved with a city that was trying to forget its broken past. Instead, I remained in the shadow of places like this. Meanwhile, to the outside world, Dundee displayed its culture and shining future, its achievements and its potential.

I had to wonder: Which was the real city?

Was it possible for both to exist side by side?

Did we only see the city we wanted to see?

What did it say about me that this was the Dundee I knew? That the shiny future so often seemed distant and unattainable to my mind. As though it belonged to other people. As though I did not deserve it.

There was movement from the kitchen. I walked through. Got to the doorway and then stepped back, my hand over my face, as a torch beam exploded in my eyes. 'Jesus!'

'You've got a hard head,' Griggs said.

'Aye, that's the truth,' a second voice said. The old man. Sounding defiant. What else would I expect? 'He's too stupid to realize when he should just give up and lie down.'

257

'Do you recognize the gun?' Griggs asked.

I blinked. The scene came into focus. Illuminated not just by the torch, but by streetlights leeching over the rear garden and through the slats in the metal covers across the windows.

I could see the dust dancing.

The old man was on his knees, facing away from Griggs, head bowed, fingers locked at the back of his skull. The SCDEA agent was holding a handgun.

Sure, I knew the gun. Why he had chosen that one in particular. Although God only knew how he got his hands on it. Maybe there was no longer anything left of the old Sandy Griggs: the man of honour and integrity. The man who had once believed completely in justice. He was so consumed by his need for revenge that nothing else mattered any more. He had given himself up to that hatred that I knew so well. He had become what I had tried so long to escape.

I said, 'Why that gun?'

'You're not daft, McNee. You can figure it out. For all the speeches you give, I know you want him dead the same as me. You've got as much reason. Jesus, he's the reason that Ernie Bright's fucking dead. Susan's too scared to face up to her anger, but you understand. You killed a man with this gun, McNee.'

I remembered the way that the bald thug had been knocked back. The way he crumpled to the muddy ground like a discarded doll.

And the way that one act of violence failed to fill the gaping, aching hole in my heart like I hoped it would.

'No,' I said. 'This isn't how it ends. We don't kill him. We can't. It makes us just as bad—'

That got him. 'Fuck you! Fuck your moral platitudes!'

'I mean it, Griggs. You've got so twisted up on all this you can't see right. You have to step back. He's finished. You've done your job. What you needed to do. We have more than enough to fuck him up for good. So let's end this the right way. No bloodshed. No more death.'

'I knew you were a spy,' Burns said. 'I knew you were working for him. But I know you're not like him, son . . . I know . . .'

'Shut up! You don't speak, old man. You don't say a fucking word.' Griggs's finger tightened round the trigger. I took in a sharp breath that stayed caught in my lungs.

'Or you'll kill me? Jesus, you don't really have it in you. You'll get someone else to do it, maybe. But when it comes down to it, Griggs, you won't kill me. The only man you ever killed was your father. And you've never been able to live with that, have you?'

'Shut up and I'll make it fast.'

'I was never afraid of violence, son,' Burns said. 'But it wasn't all that I lived for. You have a tool, you have to know how to use it properly. That's all I ever did. It was never personal. Never like this.'

'Crucifying a priest?'

'The message, not the medium.'

'You killed my sister.'

'She killed herself. I never even met her. Frankly, son, I couldn't give two shites about

259

some sad wee junkie whore who doesn't have the strength of character to pull her bloody socks up.'

'You gave her the means to destroy her own life.'

'I never met her. Never encouraged her. Never said she should shoot that shite in her veins. I didn't even know her name—'

'Her name was Catherine.'

'CeeCee,' I said, quietly. 'When she died, her name was CeeCee.'

Griggs was losing it. He trembled. That finger made to squeeze the trigger.

Burns couldn't see any of this. But he had to know what was happening.

I said, 'Her name was CeeCee, not Catherine. And she killed herself.'

Griggs let his gun arm drop. His features dropped with the shock of betrayal. He started to say something. But the words stuttered before he could form them.

The old man moved faster than I expected. He whirled round and got to his feet. He was holding a knife. I hadn't seen where it came from. He feinted, and grabbed at Griggs's gun with his left hand. Griggs let go of the gun as he fought for balance. Blood arced from the back of his hand where the knife caught him.

The old man dropped his knife. It clattered on the ground. The only sound for a moment. The gun leapt from Burns' left hand to his right. He adjusted his position with a practised air, and shot Griggs square in the forehead.

The silence that followed was crushing. Made me want to drop to my knees.

Fifty-Seven

Burns turned to look at me. He shook his head, as though what had happened was just one of those things: a tragedy, sure, but unavoidable.

'So,' he said. 'What happens now?'

'I don't know.'

'I wanted to believe you had seen the light, son. You know that?'

'But you knew?'

'About what you were up to? Oh, aye. My wife told you, didn't she?'

'She wasn't surprised to find herself in a police safe house.'

'But working with this prick?' He nodded quickly towards Griggs's corpse. 'You believed in his cause?'

'I didn't know. Far as I could tell, his operation was on the level.'

'Do you think I killed his sister?'

'Indirectly, yes.'

He shook his head. 'All this time, all the time we spent together . . . I don't know, I thought maybe . . . You get old, you get soft. That's what it is.' He shook his head. 'I killed his sister . . . so . . . you killed my nephew, then.'

He raised the gun.

I took a step back. Raised my hands. 'Come on,' I said. 'He's the one wanted you dead . . .'

'You just want me behind bars?' He didn't wait

for an answer. 'All the more reason for me to kill you, too, then.' He raised an eyebrow, prompting a response. I didn't have any to give. 'My nephew's dead because you took your eye off the ball.'

'Your nephew's dead because someone hated you enough to kill him.' Sure. Great move. Piss off the man with the gun. Something I'd made a habit of over the years. My personal version of Russian Roulette. One day my luck would run out. The bullet would be in the chamber.

He didn't lower the gun, but he didn't seem in a hurry to shoot me, either. We had all the time in the world. We were alone. Just the two of us. And the corpse.

'You've always known,' I said. 'That I was working with Griggs. So you must have known that whatever he told me, whatever lies he fed me, it was good enough for me to believe. Don't claim ignorance about it, now. I know you too well.'

He nodded. 'I have a sentimental streak. Wide as Loch Lomond, you see. Of course I fucking knew. I knew about Ernie, too. I just didn't know this wee prick here had such a hard-on for me. I thought it was just another investigation, another example of police harassment. Happens all the time. They get bored, eventually.'

'You didn't have to kill him.'

'Really? What choice did I have? Or did you have some kind of plan? Were you willing to take a bullet for me, son? Don't make me laugh. Somewhere in there, behind all the protestations, you want me dead the same way he did.

He blamed me for the death of his sister. I blame you for the death of my nephew. You blame me for Ernie's death. Swings and fucking roundabouts. Never ends. Sooner or later, someone has to end it.' He hesitated. 'In a way, I sympathize. There are nights I think maybe I was to blame. I liked Ernie. Always knew he'd turn me in if he got the chance, but all the same . . . I wouldn't have had him killed. You and I both know it was the crooked cunt ordered the trigger.'

'And Mick the Mick who pulled it,' I said. 'But you're right. We could play the blame game, keep going back and back and back, finally realize it was Jesus Christ himself killed Ernie.'

He smiled at that. A bloodless kind of smile.

'So what happens?' he said. 'Now that we're here, what happens?'

'I've watched you kill two men,' I said.

'Corroboration,' he said. 'The one man who might back you up is dead.'

'Don't,' I said. 'You've spent your life skating past the law. Making sure you can get away with what you know is wrong. You justify yourself. You make excuses and grand sounding speeches. About how you had no choice but to do some of the things you did. But you always had a choice. You were like the Zombie once. Maybe not as extreme, but then maybe the world wasn't so extreme back them. But you were a killer. A murderer. You were feared like the Devil himself.'

He said, 'The good old days.'

'Laugh all you want. That's what they were.

263

When men like you were respected, not hunted down like common criminals. When you were above the law. Un-fucking-touchable.'

'The good old days,' he repeated.

'Kill me, they'll catch you. They will link you to this murder. You know they will.'

'My days are over, son. That's what I've come to realize lately. There's no place for me in this world. Everything's changing. It was a bloody good run, though.'

'Bako's in prison,' I said. 'The war is over.'

He lowered the gun. 'Then let's do it,' he said. 'I can't come back from this. I'm too fucking old. Call it a stalemate.'

I reached out, took the weapon from him. He didn't resist. Didn't try and run. He merely accepted what was happening as though it was inevitable. As though he always knew how things would turn out. As we left, I turned to look at Griggs's corpse. Worried that it didn't make me feel a sense of loss. In my own way, I had become desensitized to violence and death.

Fifty-Eight

He wanted to say goodbye to his wife.

That was the condition. All he wanted. How could I refuse?

I called Susan. Told her this was all off the record. That we could end this peacefully if we did this on the old man's terms. She didn't try and dissuade me. She just said that she'd do it. No inflection to her voice. No emotion.

Burns told me where the meeting place would be. He said he had his reasons.

'There's something else,' Susan said, as I was about to hang up.

'What?'

'Bako.'

My stomach tightened. 'What about him?'

'It's not him. The man we locked up. We ran his fingerprints. Got back a hit fast. Maybe because we made it clear who we thought he was. But he's not the Zombie. His name is Andras Halasz. Or Halasz Andras. However you want to do it. Some Hungarian family names come before the given name. Whatever, he's ten years too young to be the Zombie. There's something wrong. I don't . . . no one's ever seen Bako, Steed. I'm beginning to wonder if he ever existed.'

Like a bedtime story. A monster in the closet.

When the police go looking, Macavity's not there.

I thought about the man I met. How he seemed a little off. And yet he had commanded authority. Made all the right noises.

I thought about him.

And the woman who had whispered in his ear.

'Did Bako have any other family?'

'Steed, I don't know the case . . . I don't . . . look, we all know he's a legend. This guy, maybe he was just taking advantage of the name. Another in a long line of chancers.'

'A sister, maybe. Something like that. Or a wife.'

'It would be tough to . . .'

'Just . . . I don't know, I'm tired, Susan. I just want . . . I just want all of this to be over.'

'What happened with Griggs?'

'We'll talk about it,' I said. 'Later.'

When I hung up, the old man said, 'Thank you.' He was belted in on the passenger's side. He sat back, his head knocking against the rest. He seemed to be struggling to even take a breath. 'Tired,' he said. 'We're all tired. I've been exhausted for years, son. Hard to believe it's all ending. But it's the old problem: when you start something, you never think about how you're going to end it. I started out on this road to stop my family from facing generations of poverty and having the shitty end of the stick handed to them. I wanted a better life. That was all. The rest of it . . .'

'Did you get it?' I turned the key, signalled. Traffic was light. The rain was starting up again. Getting heavier as it pattered on the roof of the car. 'The better life?'

'That's the thing, son. Life could always be better. So . . . I don't really fucking know.'

He closed his eyes. We drove on in silence. Something in my stomach continued to turn. A sense of expectation. Of something coming towards us.

An ending, perhaps.

A new beginning.

Something.

Fifty-Nine

The peak of the law. In the shadow of the observatory. Looking out across the city.

Where David Burns proposed to his wife.

Maybe he was being sentimental. Hoping the good memories would soften the blow of what he had to tell her. Either way, he felt it was a significant place for all of this to end. Looking out over the city he loved with the woman he loved. Accepting the inevitable change that came with age.

In some ways, this was his funeral.

Death. Prison. For a man like Burns, they weren't too far removed.

Mary was there, with Susan. Given everything she had been through, Mary looked good. A little shaky. Still hadn't had the chance to change out of the clothes she'd been wearing when we were abducted by the man who may or may not have been Zsomobor Bako.

Susan's eyes met mine as we approached on foot. A few times on the footpath, I'd felt the urge to reach out and steady the old man. He hadn't been lying about feeling old. This was the beginning of the end for him. He'd achieved everything he'd set out to do. The last few decades had been about pride, holding on to what he was because he didn't know what else to do. Now he looked ready to simply let go and move on.

Dead man walking.

Their embrace was simple and momentary. But you could feel the connection between them. Susan and I were separated by the couple, and I found that I couldn't meet her eyes across them.

'I'm sorry,' Burns said, when he stepped back. 'For everything, But especially, this . . . you were never supposed to be . . .'

'It was always the risk.'

'There were rules. Unspoken rules, but . . .'

'Young people don't have time for rules,' she said, and smiled. 'You never did.'

He nodded. She was the only person who could tell him he was wrong. It was strange to think of the old man having any kind of human connection. Even his children had tried to distance themselves from the family name and reputation. But Mary had stuck by him. The only person to ever see beyond the bluff and bluster to the human being underneath.

And he was human. Much as I – and so many others – had demonized him, the old man was as human and flawed as anyone else.

'This is sweet,' a voice said. Slight accent. But the mockery coming through clear. 'Very sweet. Beautiful. A romantic ending. I do like a romantic ending.'

I turned to see a woman step out from the shadows. Dressed in an A-line skirt and a red cardigan worn over a dark blouse. It was hard to read her expression. Her features had a natural sternness to them. The same expression I had seen on her face when she whispered into the ear of the man we had believed to be Zsomobor Bako.

But there was no Bako. I knew that, now. Maybe there never had been.

Two men flanked her. Built like tanks. I recognized one of them from the building where myself and Mary had been taken. The second was new to me, but I figured if he ever spoke, he'd have a European accent.

'Ms Bako,' I said.

She smiled. 'Very smart. You are smart, Mr McNee.'

'How long has your brother been dead?'

'My fiancé,' she said. 'So maybe not that smart. A long time. We had . . . mutual interests. It was only natural that someone fill his place.'

'But no one would accept a woman as the Zombie?'

'Feminism is a dirty word in some circles. Even today. In these enlightened times.'

Burns laughed. Loud and long. 'A woman?'

'You see what I am saying.'

'Oh, lass, if I'd known . . .'

'Precisely. But you did not know. Now you will die knowing that a woman bested you. That a woman won the war men have been fighting for years.' She was holding a gun. Small. Compact. Looked like a Sig. But what did that matter, when it would kill you just the same?

The two thugs carried Walther P7s. But of course. I knew the feel of the guns, knew that they would make these men feel powerful. The same style of gun I had used to kill a man what felt like a lifetime ago.

I let my hands go to my jacket pocket. Felt the weight in there of the gun I had carried five years

269

ago. Was it heavier now that it had a man's blood on it?

Hard to say.

I looked at Burns.

He shook his head. Saying, 'no'? Or, 'not yet'?

He looked back at the woman. 'No one has won anything, lass. Except the bastard police. Your wee scapegoat is locked up. Your business partners are dead. And as for me, fuck all of this. I'm done. I'm out.' He looked at Susan. 'My name is David Burns and I am guilty of everything you care to accuse me of. I've been a bad bastard. I've killed men. And I've had men killed. I've been a drug runner. I've run illicit gambling dens, derived money through prostitution, organized corruption and—'

'Enough! This ends tonight, Mr Burns. You will die. Your enterprises will be little more than an afterthought. A fond memory of the days when criminals played by rules. But this is a new world, Mr Burns. Without order. Without rules. The twenty-first century. No more borders. No more limits. Those who killed my fiancé, they taught me that. The rules are whatever is best for you. If you even once think about other people, you lose. No room for sentiment. No room for weakness.'

I looked at Burns again.

What was I waiting for? Permission?

He stepped forward, in front of his wife, between her and the people with guns. Showing them his sentiment. He got to his knees. 'This is it, then,' he said. 'Kill me, then, you bitch.'

She smiled, nodded to one of the thugs. The big man moved forward.

Burns turned his head to look at me. Winked. Did anyone else see it?

The heavens opened. The rain fell thick and fast. Its roar filled the space around us; an enveloping noise with a physicality all of its own. A cocoon of sound that sealed us off from the rest of the world. The rain pressed down, each drop a tiny knife pricking against my skin.

Burns adjusted his jacket. His hand slipped inside.

The knife.

He moved fast, the old energy back, as he forced the knife upwards, stabbed the thug straight in the balls. The man screamed and dropped his weapon.

I pulled the gun from my jacket and raised it. Flicked the safety with my thumb. Squeezed with my trigger finger.

The noise was deadened by the rain, but the blowback still shook my body; a deep and penetrating vibration.

The second thug had started to react, as I drew on him. He was halfway through spinning to look at me when he threw his head back and reached for his neck before collapsing to the muddy ground. Blood diluted in the rain. His eyes fluttered.

The woman raised her gun, but with at least two targets, she hesitated for just a moment. Burns was on his feet, strode forward and pressed the gun he took from the fallen thug to her head. He didn't say anything. No final words. No punchlines. This wasn't the movies or some cheap detective novel. He pulled the trigger.

As the sound of gunshots dissipated, we were left with the white noise of the rain and the low moans of the thug whose genitals had been ripped open by the old man's knife.

Burns dropped his weapon.

I held on to mine. Staring at him. Unable to believe the brutality of what I had witnessed despite everything that I knew about him.

The old man kneels before me. He spreads his arms and lowers his head . . .

Sixty

When daylight came, and the crime scene unit sealed off the area to search for evidence, two bullets would be dug out of the sodden earth just behind where the old man had been kneeling.

I could have killed him. I squeezed the trigger with intent. But at the last moment I raised the muzzle over his head. If I hadn't done that, God knows what might have happened. That old rage that had been building was looking for a release. I had given it what it demanded. But refused to give in completely.

The old man would lose his hearing for two days, but given everything he had done, that seemed lenient.

Susan arrested him, gave him the full speech about his rights, even though he barely responded. She cuffed him. Called for backup.

Mary remained silent throughout.

272

After loosing the shots, I dropped the weapon, collapsed on to the grass. My chest constricted. My arms and legs turned numb. Pins and needles. The rain seemed gentler somehow. The cool drops numbed my face like dental anaesthetic. The inside of my skull quietened. I felt at peace.

I woke up in hospital. Under observation. Susan was there. When I looked at her, she reached over and squeezed my hand.

I slept for a long time.

'You want to talk?'

DS Kellen. Sitting beside the bed, waiting for me to wake up. God only knew how long she'd been doing that.

'Depends.'

'On?'

'Whether you think I'm the bad guy.'

'Death follows you, McNee. I know that much.'

'I try not to make a habit of it.'

'Try harder.'

'Do I need a solicitor?'

'Do you think you need one?'

She produced a tape recorder. 'Just tell me everything. From the beginning.'

'That could take a while.'

'Then let's start with your name, shall we?' She hit record. 'Interview number one. Twenty-fifth November. Present in the room are DI Helen Kellen and the subject, Ja—'

The newspapers went wild. Local. National. International. The arrest of a man like David

Burns was headline news. A triumph for the forces of law and order. It was the kind of narrative that sold papers, that garnered clicks, got people talking on and off-line.

I was confined to a private room in the hospital. Three reporters managed to get in. None of them got a quote. They called me the Silent Detective.

I was happy with that.

Mitchell came to see me a few times. I gave her an edited version of what happened to Griggs. She listened, made notes and nodded a lot. She didn't believe me. That much was obvious, but there was little she could do or say. Griggs's death put a kibosh on her investigation. All she could do was clean up the pieces and try to make a narrative out of what happened.

The last time she came to see me, when she was done, her notebook closed, she looked at me and said, 'It's a neat story.'

'Too neat?'

She shook her head. 'Neat enough.'

Three days after the bloodbath at the observatory, the news broke that Mary Burns was filing for divorce. She had told me that she knew what her husband was, that she had always accepted it. But seeing it first hand was something she had never expected to happen. She had watched him mutilate a man and kill a woman without a word. Even though his actions could be argued to have been in self-defence, the look in his eyes and the lack of remorse must have rattled her.

Meaning she finally saw him as other people did.

274

I should have reached out to her, tried to show some kind of empathy.

But I never did.

What could I say to her, after all?

The trial was long and drawn-out. The defence tried to show that I had been involved in an illegal investigation and entrapment. But the man himself had admitted to his crimes. Despite the best efforts of his legal team, Burns allowed himself to be sent down. He did so in spectacular style, and I suspect he saw the trial and its fallout as part of his own punishment. If his empire was to burn, then he would be the one to light the match.

The woman who had been Zsomobor Bako's fiancée was interred as a Jane Doe. Like her intended, she had become a ghost. No one knew her real name. The man who had acted as her front refused to speak, referring to her only as 'the boss'. Her dental records and fingerprints had no known match. She died the same way she had lived; unknown, mysterious and deadly.

But rumours of the Zombie refused to die. Some people claimed that the operation continued even without someone in charge.

Cut the head off a snake, and sometimes it just keeps going.

Over the course of the trial, I admitted to my mistakes. All except one.

Three years earlier, a young girl had killed a man in a fit of rage. The man had been a psychotic killer. I had attempted to take the blame for his death, but Susan claimed to have killed him in the line of duty. And I had accepted that lie. The girl had been too traumatized to speak about the incident. I could never be sure if she really knew what had happened.

My voice shook when I spoke about the incident and how it involved David Burns, who was the Godfather of the girl. But I kept the truth to myself, all the while focussing my gaze at the back of the court, where Susan sat watching, her eyes always on me.

Sixty-One

One year later.

David Burns was serving life. In solitary. For his own protection. Rumour mill said that he was also on suicide watch.

I tried not to care.

My appeal was under consideration by the ABI in regard to my suspension. I was trying to get my business back together.

The SCDEA was disbanded, as Griggs had predicted it would be. Nothing to do with corruption but the First Minister was set on streamlining the police forces, creating a unified service: Police Scotland. No one was entirely confident about the prospect.

My work as an investigator was beginning to build again. Small scale. A few divorce cases. A couple of missing person jobs. The irony of the investigative business is that the more people know who you are, the less they want to employ you. How can you be discreet when everyone knows your face and your name?

All the same, I managed.

I was sorting notes on a missing daughter job. A local builder had employed me to find his missing girl. She had fallen in with the wrong crowd, and, one too many arguments with Dad later, decided to split. My contacts has spotted her down in Manchester where she was smoking too much weed and getting piercings. Not the worst-case scenario. The builder had gone to fetch her himself. Turned out the girl had run off after her dad remarried and spent too much doting on the wife who wasn't much older than the girl.

Teenage rebellion.

Age-old story.

But simple.

Simple was what I wanted.

The buzzer rang from the front desk. Dot told me that Susan was here. I said to send her on through.

Susan came in, sat on the edge of my desk. Dressed in civilian clothes. She'd allowed her hair to grow out, had tied it back in a loose pony tail and let some stray strands frame her face. I took her hand, stood up and kissed her.

She said, 'I'm surprised you're here today.'

'Aye?'

She nodded at the calendar.

I looked at the date.

Every year for six years on this date, I had

driven out to a lonely field in Fife and stood there, thinking about what I had lost in one night of bad decisions and bad luck.

For six years, my life had been about trying to find a way forward. A few times I had come close, but I had kept slipping. Unresolved issues holding me back.

And now?

'I hadn't noticed,' I said. 'Is that a bad thing?'

Susan shook her head. 'We all move on.'

I nodded. 'New beginnings?'

'A new story. A different one.'

She didn't say 'a better one', perhaps because we both knew it was a tough one to hope for.

New beginnings. I had been looking for one for years, but sometimes things happen only when you stop looking, when you allow yourself to be open to possibility.

I squeezed Susan's hand.

We talked about our plans for the evening.

The world moved on.

The future was filled with possibilities. More than just blood and pain. More than despair and darkness.

There was hope.

Notes and Acknowledgements

It's that time again – the bit at the back of the book no one bothers to read except the author, their family, and people they once met on the street hoping they'll sneak a mention. But it's something of a tradition, and as I've said before, it may be my name on the front of the book, but it doesn't get there without the help and support of a lot of people.

I always said I had a five book plan for McNee, and here we are. Not that it's necessarily the very end (never say die!), but certainly it brings to a close the themes and the stories I wanted to tell. It's all wound up a little different than I expected and that last scene is not the one I thought it would be, but I think perhaps it's more satisfying than if I went the obvious route. McNee has been through a lot in five books and here he is, out the other side and perhaps, finally, he's going to have a little happiness. At least, for a while.

Burns, on the other hand, well, his fate was always going to be thus. I didn't quite realise all the details, of course, and again there's one subtle difference to what happens that I think is more emotionally satisfying than the initial plan. But

279

the five books have really been about him and McNee and now, that's it. We're done.

Let me just, before we go any further, thank the city of Dundee for allowing me to play so fast and loose with my fictional version of the city and to all its citizens for your support over the years.

None of this would have been possible without so many people, so let me start with:

Mum and Dad – who still don't have that house in France but are still endlessly supportive.
Lesley McDowell – For all the best reasons . . . *J't'aime, mademoiselle.*

And move on to:
Allan Guthrie – who helped get McNee into print and more importantly helped him stay there.
Kate Lyall Grant – for allowing McNee to reach book #5 intact! Thank you for all your help and support.
Anna Telfer – who has the thankless job of whipping these books into shape; thank you for your patience and advice.
Ross Bradshaw – who was the first publisher to believe in McNee . . . and whose bookshop in Nottingham is well worth a visit!
Gail Mitchell – who made the winning bid for a cameo in this book way back in 2013 at the World Child Cancer (www.worldchildcancer.org) dinner. Brilliantly generous, and so enthusiastic; I do hope she enjoys the book!
Booksellers everywhere – the beautiful people. You are all marvellous!

Librarians everywhere – there is nothing I enjoy more than visiting a good library!

And finally, in no special order, a few people who contributed in ways they may or may not realise – moral support, plot suggestions, answering daft questions and just buying me a pint: Robert Simon Macduff Duncan, Jay Stringer, Dave White, Charlie Stella, The Booksellers (past and present) at Waterstones Dundee and Newton Mearns (far too many of you to list, but you know who you are!), the red and blue shirts from Bookworld (again, so many brilliant people, so little word count!), Ross McLean, Linda Landrigan, Jon Jordan, Ruth Jordan, Jen Jordan, Janet Boyle, Chris Ewan, James Oswald, Stuart MacBride, Gary Smith, Kimberley Smith, Becca Simpson, and, of course, Moriarty McDowell-McLean (I can't believe I acknowledged a cat, but it just goes to show that writing eventually sends you completely mad).

Anyone I missed out – and there will be someone, there's always someone – because frankly I have a Swiss cheese memory. But you know who you are. And you know what you've done!

And of course, the readers. All of you. Thank you for your support and kind words. Even those of you who think I use far too many naughty words.